Henry Edwards Pardee

# Statistics of the Class of 1856, of Yale College

Anatiposi

Henry Edwards Pardee

# Statistics of the Class of 1856, of Yale College

Reprint of the original, first published in 1859.

1st Edition 2023 | ISBN: 978-3-38231-246-6

Anatiposi Verlag is an imprint of Outlook Verlagsgesellschaft mbH.

Verlag (Publisher): Outlook Verlag GmbH, Zeilweg 44, 60439 Frankfurt, Deutschland
Vertretungsberechtigt (Authorized to represent): E. Roepke, Zeilweg 44, 60439 Frankfurt, Deutschland
Druck (Print): Books on Demand GmbH, In de Tarpen 42, 22848 Norderstedt, Deutschland

# STATISTICS

OF

# THE CLASS OF 1856,

OF

# YALE COLLEGE,

COLLECTED BY

## HENRY EDWARDS PARDEE,

CLASS SECRETARY.

Published by Order of the Class.

NEW HAVEN:
TUTTLE, MOREHOUSE & TAYLOR, PRINTERS.

1859.

"A chance remark —a pictured face—a name—
A thousand things we do not dream of now,
Will serve as talismans of memory,
To bring these old associations back:
So shall we live this student life again,
And old companions, with their hearty grasps,
And shouts and songs, and slow ascending smoke,
Will fill the pictures of our happy dream."

*Buehler's Class Poem.*

# PREFACE.

———•—•———

My Classmates :—The arrangement of the Class Report was completed several weeks since. I have delayed the publication in order to insert any additional items that might come to hand. It does not seem advisable, however, to wait longer, and those, therefore, who have omitted to write to me, must now climb to immortality by some other path.

It is hardly to be expected that the Report is free from mistakes. It was no small task to collect these statistics; but if every man had taken one ninety-sixth as much pains as I have, to make them full and accurate, we might easily have thrown the rest of the blame on the printer. I earnestly request that any one who discovers errors or omissions, will inform me of them, so that I can make the necessary changes on the Secretary's book.

I have been much gratified at the interest in my progress which many of the Class have manifested. I am under especial obligation to Messrs. J. M. Brown, Catlin, Coit, Cowles, and Packard, for their prompt assistance in getting statistics. Many thanks are also due to Mr. Josiah W. Harmar, of the Class of '55, for useful suggestions in regard to the Triennial Meeting.

It is desirable that you communicate to the Secretary all events in your lives which would be of interest to any of your Classmates, such as change of residence or business, marriage, and the birth of children, appointments, promotions, &c. All such facts, that come to my knowledge through newspapers, business cards, letters, or reliable report, I shall insert in the Secretary's Book. You are all invited to consult it at any time for such information as it may contain.

In the hope that it may tend to strengthen the bonds that unite us, I respectfully submit this Report to the Class of 1856, and with earnest wishes for the success and happiness of each, I subscribe myself,

Your Obedient Servant,

HENRY E. PARDEE.

NEW HAVEN, Sept. 27, 1859.

# CLASS MEETINGS BEFORE GRADUATING.

It may be pleasing to the class to be reminded of some of our early meetings. We were assembled for the first time in the College Chapel, at 11 A. M., on the 16th of September, 1852, for the purpose of being assigned to our respective divisions, and started on our course. Professor Hadley remarked, on dismissing the meeting, that it was customary with the Faculty to insist on absolute punctuality—a suggestion which exerted a marked influence on the class through College. Sept. 21st the class had a meeting, the purpose of which seemed to be to call out those who were said to be good speakers ; Oct. 5th the President addressed us on our duties and privileges ; Oct. 6th another meeting ; Oct. 9th a meeting to challenge the Sophomores to the foot-ball game ; on the 12th a meeting to talk about it ; on the 13th, at noon, a meeting to complete arrangements, and at four P. M., a crowded meeting with the Sophs on the foot-ball ground ; Oct. 26th Professor Silliman, Senior, addressed us on personal habits. After this we always had meetings whenever a reasonable excuse could be presented. The last undergraduate meeting was held in the Brothers' Hall, July 29th, 1856, when E. A. Walker, Cowles and Pardee, were appointed Class Committee.

# CLASS MEETINGS SINCE GRADUATING.

## FIRST MEETING.

Twenty-two of the class, who happened to be in the vicinity, met at the end of the Spring Term, 1857, and spent an exceedingly pleasant evening in the old way, with music, song and story.

## SECOND MEETING.

About thirty of the class met in Professor Porter's Recitation Room, on the evening of Wednesday, July 29th, 1857. Each one gave an account of his year's experience, and answered categorically and conscientiously to the five queries : whether married, engaged, in love, thinking about it, or indifferent.

## THIRD MEETING.

About twenty of the class met on the grass in front of North Middle, at the Commencement of 1858.— Messrs. Paine and Wilcox were added to the committee.

## TRIENNIAL MEETING.

To those of us who lived in New Haven, it seemed like the end of another long vacation, when the class of '56 came back to attend this meeting. It is unne-

cessary to attempt a description of the hearty saluta-
tions, the mutual inquiries, the groups of smiling faces,
the ringing laugh as some joke renewed its age, the up-
roarious flocking here and there, as each new comer
dawned on us, or of jolly crowds filing off to old resorts.
Those who have seen few classmates' faces in the past
three years, can imagine with how much zest they
would have entered into the hilarity of fifty fifty-sixers,
bound to have a good time. There were present fifty-
four members, viz: Messrs. Arnot, B. F. Barker,
Brewer, H. B. Brown, J. M. Brown, T. Brown, Buehler, Bulkeley, Bushee, Calkins, Campbell, Catlin, Clark,
Coit, Condit, Cowles, Denniston, Depew, Dorrance,
Dow, Dunlap, Fiske, French, Gay, Harriott, Hodge,
Hoppin, Johnson, Keeler, Kinzer, Lamson, McIntire,
Mann, Monteith, Morse, Nettleton, Packard, Paine,
Pardee, Peck, Righter, Robinson, Smith, Steinman,
Swayne, Taylor, Town, Turner, Webb, Whitney, Wilcox, Wilkinson, Woods, Worrall. Campbell was pre-
vented by sudden illness from attending the evening
meeting, and Robinson was unable to stay all night.—
Harris was unexpectedly called out of town before the
meeting. Eight of those who left the class before graduation, accepted the invitation to be present at the meeting, viz : Messrs. Bacon, Colt, Hulbert, Kimball, Ma-
gill, S. T. C. Merwin, Northrop, St. John, making in
all sixty-one who sat down to the table.

On Wednesday, July 27th, at 12 M., the class held a
preliminary meeting at the President's Lecture Room.
Father Worrall presided. Chauncey M. Depew, of
Peekskill, N. Y., was unanimously chosen the President
of the evening meeting. It was announced, very much
to the regret of all present, that Emmett A. Eakin, to

whose daughter we had determined to present the Silver Cup, would be unable to attend the re-union. A
resolution was then offered that we present a Silver
Cup, at the next general meeting, to the oldest boy
born to any member of the class. An amendment was
offered that a preference should be given to those not
then married, and as amended, the motion was carried.
The Secretary announced that the entire expenses of
the meeting would require of each five dollars and three
quarters, payable at the table,—absentees being taxed
a dollar each towards paying expenses of the report.
The meeting was interrupted by a visit from Mr. Staf-
ford, the Printer, who, in a manner "*plain*" rather
than "*ornamental*," presented a document for inspec-
tion.

The meeting adjourned at 1 o'clock. At 9 o'clock, P.
M., we assembled again at the President's Lecture
Room, and at fifteen minutes before 10, started for the
New Haven House, singing Gaudeamus. We stopped
on the way to cheer the Yale Boat Club, who had that
day beaten Harvard at Worcester, and who were having a bonfire in the College yard. Then, to the tune of
" A jolly set of Bricks, Sir," we entered the Hotel and
took our places at the table at 10 o'clock. A blessing
was asked by "Deacon" Taylor. The company then
proceeded to act upon the bill of fare, which no one un-
derstands preparing better than Mr. Allis. Meanwhile
the committee made the circuit of the tables, and received from each his quid pro quo. Our proceedings
were slightly interrupted by the class of 1853, who astonished us by marching into the room, bearing at
their head their class boy, and presenting him as a
worthy candidate for our cup. We concluded, how-

ever, to wait, consoling ourselves with the reflection
that the boy we had was made for a higher sphere,
that the boys we have are girls, and hoping that the
boy we shall have will be as fair a match for their fine
fellow as the class of '56 has been, in other respects, to
the class of '53. After ample justice had been done to
the viands, we sang—

### GAUDEAMUS.

Gaudeamus igitur,
  Juvenes dum sumus ;
Post jucundam juventutem,
Post molestam senectutem,
  Nos habebit humus.

Ubi sunt, qui ante nos
  In mundo fuere ?
Transeas ad superos,
Abeas ad inferos,
  Quos si vis videre.

Vita nostra brevis est,
  Brevi finietur ;
Venit mors velociter,
Rapit nos atrociter,
  Nemini parcetur.

Vivat academia
  Vivant professores,
Vivat membrum quodlibet,
Vivant membra, quælibet,
  Semper sint in flore.

Vivant omnes virgines,
  Faciles, formorsæ,
Vivant et mulieres,
Teneræ, amabiles,
  Bonæ laboriosæ.

Pereat tristitia,
  Pereant osores,
Pereat diabolus,
Quivis antiburschius,
  Atque irrisores.

Quis confluxus hodie,
  Academicorum ?
E longinquo convenerunt
Protinusque successerunt
  In commune forum.

Alma Mater floreat,
  Quæ nos educavit,
Caros et commilitones
Dissitas in regiones
  Sparsos congregavit.

The President of the meeting then made the following
remarks :

It is a source of congratulation, gentlemen, that we are gathered
in such goodly numbers here to-night. It is indicative of the fact
that the spirit and enthusiasm which, from Foot-Ball to Commencement, from matriculation to graduation, so eminently distinguished in
College, still characterizes the Class of '56. It is also a source of un-
feigned thankfulness that death, who spares neither beauty nor age,

2

and visits with destroying hand both the cottage and the palace, while committing his ravages on every side of us, scattered as we were all over this country and in foreign lands, has passed us by untouched, and left our numbers undiminished—our phalanx unbroken—from Arnot to Worrall a united whole ; and that if we have any cause for grief at this time, it is not for a man who has gone out of, but for a boy who has not been born into, the world !

Our old enmities buried, our old loves renewed, all that separated us forgotten, and all that bound us together rendered dearer by the mellow light of memory, we come with our three years' experience of active life, of battle, of victory, or of defeat, to re-visit these scenes of our early struggles and joys—where every building and room and street, every elm and nook and walk, where the shadows which fall from the twin rocks, and the waves which dance in the bay, have each and all a silent history and suggestive interest. We come to re-call those strifes, the recollection of which, as is usual and noble with worthy foemen, knits us closer now as generous friends ; to recount our struggles and adventures, and to bid each other God-speed for a longer and more arduous pilgrimage.

During this period, the members of our class have not been idle.— Some have proved themselves able and earnest men, have done brave service and won enviable reputations in the pulpit, and, by precept and example, " allured to brighter worlds and led the way." Others have already mastered the arduous profession of the law, and risen to honorable positions at the bar. Others have put their impress upon the public opinion of the nation, making the welkin ring from Maine to California, with their eloquent appeals to the American, the Republican and the Democratic masses. Others still have been successful in securing for themselves that material wealth which, if the love of it is the root of all evil, the experience of most of us has doubtless proved that the possession of it is exceedingly convenient. While a choice few have been studying Law at Heidelburgh, Theology at Berlin, Art in Italy, and one, at least, has been selling peanuts and acquiring the title of " The Black Ruffian," on the plains of Kansas.

But we are especially interested here, to-night, in the laurels won in the lists of love. I well remember the eager promise which we all made, as we shook hands upon the College green, at the earliest opportunity to fulfill the first duty of an American citizen, and an Alumnus of Yale ; and often did we pledge ourselves in the swinging chorus of—

" Roll the song in waves along
For the hours are bright before us,
And in cottage and vale are the brides of Yale,
Like Angels waiting for us."

But I am sorry to state that most of them are still waiting ; and if, not only in poetry but in fact, such beings are in existence, unless we are more faithful in the future than our past gives promise, I fear they will continue to wait until their sweetness becomes most acidly spinster. All honor, then, to the glorious little band who have done their part toward redeeming the credit of the class ! Long life and peace and domestic happiness be theirs ! And to us, (I speak like a penitent,) who have been wandering over the arid plains and barren hills of bachelor life, whatever our sufferings, and if ever so great— though we have longed for those soothing appliances which are a sovereign remedy—though the dust has gathered thick on the books of our libraries—though choice articles clipped with care, to be methodically preserved, are now a hopeless chaos—though our buttons, like Peggotty's hooks and eyes, are forever flying off—though our garments are crying aloud for some Eve to sew the tears—though generally dilapidated, uncared for and forsaken—to us, unless we amend, be the secondary position, but oft repeated responsibility of sponsors and God-Fathers.

This is an occasion, gentlemen, such as happens to a man but once or twice in a life-time ; an event which makes an era in our history ; one of those rare seasons of hearty reunion and of mutual confidences, when, in the complete outpouring and unburthening of our whole selves—in the melting and fusing of all that is individual and selfish, we can feel, from the depths of our being, a true, manly, earnest, and honest emotion. As each one of us is to be profited by the experience of all the rest, so is each to be, of all the rest, the repository of cherished secrets. If disappointment or sorrow has happened to any, it is our privilege to hear it, for it is the misfortune of us all. If great success has crowned the efforts of any, it is not egotism to relate it, for it is the common property and the common glory of us all. And I feel assured that whatever these utterances may be, whether responses to sentiments or chapters from life, whether the details of action or the expressions of thought, they will prove that the class of '56 is not unworthy to take its place among the worthiest of those who have gone forth from Alma Mater Yale.

After the President's Speech, we sang the Alumni Song, by F. M. FINCH, of the class of '49 :

*AIR—" Sparkling and Bright."*

Gather ye smiles from the ocean isles,
   Warm hearts from river and fountain,
A playful chime from the palm tree clime,
   From the land of rock and mountain ;
     And roll the song in waves along,
       For the hours are bright before us,
     And grand and hale are the elms of Yale,
       Like fathers, bending o'er us.

Summon our band from the prairie land,
   From the granite hills, dark frowning,
From the lakelet blue, and the black bayou,
   From the snows our pine peaks crowning ;
     And pour the song in joy along,
       For the hours are bright before us,
     And grand and hale are the towers of Yale,
       Like giants, watching o'er us.

Count not the tears of long gone years,
   With their moments of pain and sorrow,
But laugh in the light of their memories bright,
   And treasure them all for the morrow.
     Then roll the song in waves along,
       While the hours are bright before us,
     And high and hale are the spires of Yale,
       Like guardians towering o'er us.

Dream of the days when the rainbow rays
   Of Hope on our hearts fell lightly,
And each fair hour some cheerful flower
   In our pathway blossomed brightly ;
     And pour the song in joy along
       Ere the moments fly before us,
     While portly and hale the sires of Yale
       Are kindly gazing o'er us.

Linger again in memory's glen,
   'Mid the tendrilled vines of feeling,
Till a voice or a sigh floats softly by,
   Once more to the glad heart stealing ;
     And roll the song in waves along,
       For the hours are bright before us,
     And in cottage and vale are the brides of Yale,
       Like angels watching o'er us.

Clasp ye the hand 'neath the arches grand
That with garlands span our greeting,
With a silent prayer that an hour as fair
May smile on each after meeting;
And long may the song, the joyous song
Roll on in the hours before us,
And grand and hale may the elms of Yale
For many a year bend o'er us.

The President then announced the first regular toast of the evening, " Our Alma Mater," to which JOHN MONTEITH responded as follows :

MR. CHAIRMAN AND BROTHER CLASSMATES :—There is a propriety in my addressing you as *brother* classmates. For what other title could I use when I speak to you of our Alma Mater ?

No accident has conferred upon our beloved institution this classic epithet. Our Alma Mater is the common parent of our intellectual fitness. The calumniator of liberal education tauntingly asks, how much of Latin sentences and Greek roots we remember, now that we have been absent from these classic shades for three years. But he forgets that it was the sole business of our mother to give to our intellects Herculean strength and brawny muscle, while the " beeves and loaves " that nourished, may long since have been consumed and forgotten. She gave us no ornaments. These were to be the reward of hearty zeal, and patient industry. She sent us from her embrace, as God sent our first Parents from the Garden—clad in the skins of animals. Hence it is, sir, that while the sons of Harvard are intellectual gentlemen, the sons of Yale are *intellectual men.*

Our Alma Mater is, to a great degree, the parent of our success.— Age and deserving honor never fail to contribute a respectability to the family, which is sure to be communicated to all its members. One hundred and fifty-nine years have rolled over the head of our mother, and given her silvery locks, and each departing year has laid new laurels at her feet. From these she has always freely imparted to her sons ; so that whatever might be our *real* worth, we could always claim the *prestige* of a *good family.*

To our Alma Mater we owe a tribute of gratitude for all those tender ties of friendship which bind us together as classmates. Those who are attracted to common objects of affection, must be drawn closely to each other.

The recitation rooms, those old buildings which have so often rung with our mirth, those old elms, so often the music halls of our united song, were hardly more than the scenes of our growing friendships.— The recitations because they were honored, the buildings and elms because they were old, have made those attachments all the more deep and enduring.

The Faculty of our Alma Mater are a crown of palms to her gray locks. The restraints they imposed upon us we regard *now*, as *whippings* simply, designed for our ultimate good. After all, we are bound to acknowledge that we love our old instructors. Their eminence, their efforts to give us sound learning, and the personal interest which they have taken in each one of us, have endeared them to us. One has gone. His kind instructions, his gentlemanly bearing, and his friendly familiarity, gained our friendship and esteem. We shall always cherish with pleasure, the memory of our lamented Professor Olmsted.

Our Alma Mater extends her guardian care over our active life.— Her object in training us was, that we might be *men*. She desired that we should mingle our spirit with the spirit of the age. She sent us out to fight the battles of useful life. And now I can imagine her, with the proud anxiety of a Grecian mother, looking in upon this scene, and putting the question to each one of us, " My son, these three years thou hast been absent from my embrace, what hast thou done for the age—for the world ?"

Thus the benefits we derive from our Alma Mater, extend over our past and our future. For these benefits—never more dear to us than to-night—we will hand down to posterity those praises which have so often filled our song :

" Alma Mater, Alma Mater, heaven's blessings attend her,
While we live, we will cherish, protect and defend her."

Next was sung the following song, written by THERON BROWN :

*AIR—" O Carry me 'long."*

Ho, back again, boys
And where and how have you been ?
Sure ye're lookin' the same but a bit more grim
And a trifle more hair to the chin.

Has the world been usin' you well ?
There's a wrinkle on some 'o yer brows,
And time and care have whitened a hair
On some of your manly pows.

> CHORUS—O ! boys, welcome ye home !
> Our hearts together are bound,
> In the " silver cup " fill a bumper up,
> And sing Triennial round.

From field and counter and bar,
From the pulpit and pedagogue's stall,
We come once more 'neath the elms of yore,
To give Alma Mater a call.
We've bro't our darlings along—
The bride in her honey-moon weeks,
And the young mamma ; hurra, hurra,
For the wives of Fifty-six !

> CHORUS—O, boys, &c.

Hail, Son* of the Class !
First-born of a myriad more,
One health to the sire who owns thee, boy !
And three to the mother who bore !
Then ho ! for a jubilee-night,
Let the feast and the fun flow on,
We're right well met ; and an hour more yet
For the days that are over and gone.

> CHORUS—O, boys, welcome ye home !
> Our hearts together are bound,
> In the silver cup fill a bumper up
> And sing Triennial round. .

The next toast announced, was "The class of '56—its Past," to which P. W. CALKINS made the following extempore remarks :

MR. PRESIDENT AND GENTLEMEN :—If any other toast than the one just read, had been assigned me by your committee this morning, I should not have ventured to intrude upon you the thoughts that could be thrown together in so brief a time. But with a sentiment that thrills my whole nature at its very mention, I feel like congratulating you, that you are to listen to no words penned in a cooler moment, but are to supply me with your own animating thoughts.— " The *Past* of '56 ! " What inspiring associations cluster around the

---

* The verse and the sentiment require " Son."—The fates and the facts insist upon the reading of " daughter."

word *past*. In a nation, and in our smaller nation, the university, the past has been the prophet of the present. Not only its associations, but its doings and its purposes, all have looked forward to an hour like this, when theories should be facts, and hopes achievements. Above all, *our own* past, is linked most holily with the present. And as we to-night live again in its dreamy presence—we bring every treasury that was real to us then, and make it doubly real now.

At the thought of the real treasures of the past, a comical vision has risen before me—which will not vanish till you all have seen it. It is the vision of *College Humbugs, sells, scrapes,* or whatever term the technical vocabulary of College may bestow upon those loads that are forever being played upon the verdant Freshman. If any of you have a copy of the *Banner*, which in 1852 led us to the field of battle, you will find a piece of advice in the following paternal style—to " the young gentlemen who have recently, &c."—

" Above all, my young friends, let me advise you never to attempt to throw off that delicious *greenness*, so eminently becoming your position, and so suggestive of the hills from which most of you have come."

That advice, I confess I followed most implicitly. Witness the old brown coat, and the shocking old beaver—which held out against your hard knocks until forbearance ceased to be a virtue. Witness the long arguments with astonished Tutors, on original demonstrations of Euclid. Witness shipwrecks on the harbor—unappreciated performances on the flute in North Middle—lugging Alumni's carpet bags from the depot in electioneering time—*et id omne genus*. Yet, though I was then one of the greenest and awkwardest of us all, I confess there is nothing that I look back upon with more unmingled delight, than upon those very "sells" of which I was the victim. And when I see similar victims coming up Chapel street, with their numerous and faithful escort, instead of feeling for them the humane sentiment of the classic Queen—

Non ignara mali, miseris succurrere disco—

I heartily congratulate them on this favorable entrance upon College life.

For, gentlemen, there is a philosophy in this matter of College Humbug. There is a scholarly and christian use to be made of the Epicurean text, *Dum vivimus vivamus*. For we may let this teach us to pour into the life of every day so much of the deepest energies of the soul that it shall become *real life*. College is the last place to live merely in hopes, and the future. There is enough that is real and earnest to make the present an all absorbing life. For every day, you know, we live two lives. One is our *routine life*, in which we do as a matter of course the things given us to do; the other is our *real life*. It comes forth from the deepest place of the soul, and goes bounding on to some great purpose, with such a gathering in of the mightiest energies, and warmest impulses, and holiest motives, that it swells the meager achievements of a day, into the intellectual wealth of an age. Now it is not possible to live this real life, without calling familiarly into exercise these deepest energies of the spirit; and animating as our literary pursuits are, they have always fallen into a dull routine, and failed in this radical work of intellectual culture, unless judiciously mingled with relaxations that are fully up to the exhilaration which we here constantly need. This is what I claim for our College *humbugs*. Although I have the greatest respect for those dear old grandmothers who go through College in such a dignified way that they never *get sold*, yet I would not give, for all their serenity, the genial enthusiasm which my own innumerable *loads* have imparted to my whole life. College humbugs, when well improved, enable us to make this our practical philosophy : *Build life upon experience, not upon theory*.

But not only for College humbugs, but for College *quarrels*, even, I claim a use. Here again I am admirably suited for the work you have given me to-night. Here, close at my right hand, sits a man who wrote as follows in my Autograph Book :—

    "*Dear Calk*,"—

"Freshman year I used to think all Linonians and Sigma Delta men devils incarnate, and *you, the arch fiend of both*."

Yet long before we separated, Jim and I were the best of friends. And I'm not afraid to look every man of you in the eye to-night, and ask you if you don't value every *true thing* that is in me, tenfold more because you so honestly and frankly quarreled with the many crotchety things you had to encounter. There was a manliness in our little animosities, which only made them a grand means of finding out the real thing that was in us. And I thank God, we have not got to say, what is almost every year repeated at this table, that we bury *now* all those animosities. We did bury them—long before that last pipe of peace was smoked, and that last press of hands was felt. And not a ghost of them can be summoned from the vasty deep to-night, to break in upon the unbroken affection of these brothers.

And that brings me to the *pleasant memories* of the past—to that largest chapter in our history, teeming with friendships unbroken by a

3

single misunderstanding—friendships tested by the holy trial of sepa-
ration, and sealed to-night for eternity ! As you called that roll, Mr.
Secretary, and face after face came up in each memory, how many
histories were recorded by our attending angels ; histories of faithful-
ness and that generous love which man may feel to one who is alto-
gether brotherly to his soul. And *all*, thank God, *all* who parted from
us with the full course of study complete, either responded with a
joyous "Here !" to your call, or sent a greeting and a cheer from the
land of the living. But—four who began with us, as full of hope,
will be starred on our first book. One we ourselves laid to rest on a
summer day, in a grove of flowers. Another has since fallen at his
post at home ; while two have been cut down on distant wanderings,
and now one of them sleeps in the wilds of South America, and the
other on the Plains of Kanzas. But the moistened eye at the
thought of death, shows that it has approached still nearer. How
many of us, during this little past, which since '52 can be called *our*
past as a class, have felt the cold hand upon the dearest treasures of
the heart—a brother—a mother—a sister. I might repeat every name
that the heart holds dear, and a tear would fall for each. And even
the sacredest name God has given to the treasures of earth, the name
of *wife*, cannot be breathed to-night, save in that subdued voice that
is sweet to the *mourner's* ear. How truthfully our thoughts to-night
reproduce the picture of the poet of sadness :—

> " Stately trees are growing,
>    Lusty winds are blowing,
>    And mighty rivers flowing
>        On, forever on ;

> " As stately forms were growing,
>    As lusty spirits blowing,
>    And as mighty fancies flowing,
>        On, forever on ;

> " But there has been leave taking,
>    Sorrow and heart breaking,
>    And a moan, pale echo's waking,
>        For the gone, forever gone.

> " Lovely stars are gleaming,
>    Bearded lights are streaming,
>    And glorious suns are beaming,
>        On, forever on ;

" As lovely eyes were gleaming,
 As wondrous thoughts were streaming,
 And as glorious minds were beaming,
  On, forever on ;

" But there has been soul sundering,
 Wailing and sad wondering,
 For the grave grows fat with plundering
  The gone, forever gone.

" We see great eagles soaring,
 We hear deep oceans roaring,
 And sparkling fountains pouring,
  On, forever on ;

" As lofty souls were soaring,
 As sonorous voices roaring,
 And as sparkling wits were pouring,
  On, forever on ;

" But pinions have been shedding,
 And voiceless darkness spreading ;
 Such a measure *death's* been treading,
  O'er the gone, forever gone !

" Every tie is sundering,
 Every one is wondering,
 And this huge world goes thundering
  On, forever on ;

" But 'mid this weary sundering,
 Heart breaking and sad wondering,
 And this huge world's rude thundering,
  On, forever on,—

" How fondly *we* are dreaming,
 Of the spot where flowers are gleaming,
 And the long, green grass is streaming,
  O'er *the gone, forever gone !*"

In the mellow light of the evening of this world, and the dawn of eternity, a new sacredness falls upon our old College friendships, which can now so perfectly make our brothers' sorrows and joys our own. I have somewhere read a delightful Persian legend, which seems to characterize very happily the friendships of this circle. It relates that among the shades in the islands of the blest, was one who instinctively shrank from his companions, and could never mingle his sensitive nature with theirs. But one day he was led by an unseen impulse, through a secluded path, to a garden of surpassing beauty. It was surrounded by an impassable hedge; something prompted him to attempt to climb it, when lo! it vanished at his touch, and with unimpeded step he passed within the enclosure. In the course of his wandering among the wonders of sight, and fragrance, and melody, he came to what appeared to be the crowning excellence of the garden. But here again a cold and sullen stream cut off his approach. Emboldened by his former experience, he drew near, and the waters divided, and he passed through without a chill. Once within the fascinating retreat, a change began to come over his whole nature. The flowers and music no longer seemed to be merely admired, but to steal into his soul with a strange power of their own. And when at last he stood before a flower of wondrous loveliness, he was conscious that its own celestial influences were transforming his very nature. Full of the new life he had here breathed, he returned to his companions. Their presence no longer seemed forbidding. Virtue went out from him as it had from the celestial blossom, and transformed their souls too. A new brotherhood was made for him. Then the shades knew that he had stood in the presence of the Flower of Eternal Friendship!

My classmates! did not some of *us* find that flower in our wanderings beneath these sacred shades? And as we approached the heart of a brother, did not the forbidding hedges of envy, and the cold streams of mistrust fade away, and seem only the creatures of our own fancies? And did not we find in that heart, not only beauty and melody to admire, but a mysterious power, to send us forth to a larger companionship in the world, with a readier access than we ever had before to the hearts of our fellow beings?

And that influence, I feel assured, we shall carry with us as we go forth again, with renewed strength. And we shall use it for sacred purposes. I doubt if I stand in the presence of a man, to-night, whose selfish ambitions tower above his purposes of good to others. We go back to our varied work, mature in the strength our Alma Mater has given us, rich in the affections of strong and true men, to lay all these treasures of mind and heart upon an altar erected to no strange people, and to no unknown God. Be this our watchword forever:—

> " Be good, my boys, and let who will be clever,
>    Do noble things, not dream them all day long,
> And so make life, death, and that vast forever,
>    One grand, sweet song!"

[Mr. Calkins offered in conclusion the following toast :]

"Our College *Enthusiasm!* The noble impulse it has imparted to our lives, proves the true etymology of the word :—*God within us!*"

Then was sung the following song, written by G. W. BUEHLER :

*AIR—" God save the Queen."*

Once more united here,
'Mid scenes we all hold dear,
    Greet we our Class—
In all our scattered homes,
Low cots and lofty domes—
Where'er a classmate roams,
    God bless our Class.

Health to our absent ones !
Whom busy memory runs
    Glad to recall—
Where'er in distant lands
This night a brother stands,
Clasping his unpressed hands,—
    God bless them all.

Old friends here greet us yet,
But friends we'll ne'er forget,
    Rest cold and pale.
Oh! while our songs ascend,
Must strains of sadness blend,
And mournful mem'ries tend,
    To graves of Yale.

Our Alma Mater! thee,
Peace and prosperity
    Shall never fail.
Memory shall linger long
Thy charmed scenes among,
And oft inspire the song,
    God save old Yale !

The next toast was, "The Wives of '56," to which S. F. WOODS made the following response :

"I confess—Mr. Chairman, and Classmates—that I can not perceive by what rule of adaptation you have seen fit to evoke from me, the

youngest member of the Class present, and of confirmed bachelor pro-
clivities, a response to the sentiment just proposed.

And peculiarly do I regret, that my untutored, dissonant words are
to follow that rare eloquence which still lingers in our ears, and that
it is my ungracious lot to disturb the weird-like charm of that voice
which, I think, charmed us "never so wisely" before.

It is possible, sir, that my well-known youth and innocent simplicity
may have been taken into consideration, with the tacit assumption of
the old principle, "Omne ignotum pro magnifico,"—and that our accom-
plished Secretary—who is I presume responsible for my appearance
before you in this unaccustomed capacity—may have thought that
Matrimony was to me such an "*ignotum*," that I should look upon
every married man of the Class as a "magnifico" of the most magnif-
icent description.

It is true, one other reason why I am called upon might suggest
itself, only to be rejected, which is, the idea that one whose knowledge
of matrimony is derived solely from limited and occasional observation,
will be likely to draw a more flattering sketch of connubial felicity,
than could those who are "behind the scenes," and who know by practical experience the sad contrast between the actual discords of wed-
lock and its ideal melody.

If my memory of the pre-collegiate classics is accurate, it was one
of the indispensables of the Eleusinian Initiations that the candidate
should take most solemn oaths of secresy before looking upon the
mysteries ; and I believe that the initiated returned to Athens, after
the ceremony, amid admiring crowds and envious, garlanded and fan-
tastically decked with horns and banners, greeting with jests and ridi-
cule those who were still strangers to the sacred mysteries.

It is in some such way, as I conceive, that the Benedicts among us
comport themselves, robed in secresy for the purpose of exciting curi-
osity or imitation, and when we, poor bachelors, dare to "lift up our
insect trump against the awful roar of their tremendous hymn," and
to say a word in favor of single blessedness, we are silenced with
laughter and jests, by those who bear the recent "cornucopiæ" of
matrimony. But I am not vindictive, and if I can say anything by
way of comfort or consolation to those of our number "who," as
Francis Bacon says, "have given hostages to Fortune, and are bur-
dened with impediments to great enterprizes, either of virtue or mis-
chief,"—if I can suggest anything which shall cast over the sad
monotony of their lives a varying smile, like the transient ripple upon

long prairie plains, gone in an instant but affording a short relief as it passes on—if thus much, I shall be fortunate.

The brief experience of a briefless lawyer can of course furnish to the eulogy of married life only the results of a very limited observation, and even that, alas! too often employed upon its shady side.

But, assuredly, orange blossoms are not to be disdained, nor the Hymeneal songs refused because Patrick and Bridget, *haud secus ac feles, amant pugnaciter*, and dissolve their wedding pearls in vinegar before the expiration of the honeymoon—or because an unhappy bridegroom comes to me to inquire whether the cold feet of his beloved wife constitute a competent ground of divorce. Such evils do not concern *us*. Rather, gentlemen, you who are married, I mean—whose "joys are divided and whose sorrows are doubled"—as somebody somewhere says. Turn from such contemplations and the malicious inferences which cynical and envious bachelors will draw therefrom, and congratulate yourselves that at least the criminal statistics of the country are in your favor, assuring us as they do that three fourths of the persons annually committed to prison in this country are bachelors.

Remember that the authorities of the past are with you—that Lycurgus in his Spartan Code provided that criminal proceedings might be instituted against those who married too late, or unsuitably, and still more severely against those who did not marry at all,—that Solon looked upon compulsory marriages with approbation,—and that by the Laws of Plato, a man who did not marry before the age of thirty-five was subject to a *mulct* and to a species of modified disfranchisement.

Remember too, that even in this 19th century, and in one of our own states, there has been a *tax* on bachelors, and that not a *poll tax*, but a special *tariff* as upon an article of useless superfluity. Remember that, in the language of Lycurgus, "these regulations were founded on the well-recognized principle that it is the duty of every good citizen to raise up a strong and healthy progeny of legitimate children to the state;" and that Plato expressly says, that "in choosing a wife every one ought to consult the interests of the commonwealth, and not his own pleasure."

Remember these things, and that in nine cases out of ten it is only an ignoble and cowardly fear of expense which prevents us all from following your example,—and the eulogistic mentions of celibacy which are frequently addressed to you, are founded on the ancient and established philosophy first introduced in the entertaining fable of the Fox and the Grapes.

But seriously, sir, I conceive that we of the Class of 1856 ought to recognize with especial honor "the *Wives of the Class.*" I know, sir, what is probably in your mind in this connection. I see it in the look of tender reproach with which you are mentally arraigning these ladies on the charge of disappointing our just and reasonable anticipations. I shall not attempt to extenuate their plea of "Guilty." In spite of the efforts of our excellent host, as seen in the elegant banquet before us, the Cup is absent, "the cup which cheers but not inebriates," and for that our joy is turned into heaviness. I do not plead in palliation, but simply ask that sentence may be suspended for three years longer, trusting that the parable of the barren fig tree will by that time have become inapplicable, and that after so long a night a *son* may dawn upon us.

The ancients were accustomed to rejoice in the birth of children, especially that they thereby should have those who would cast flowers upon their tombs and perform for them sepulchral rites. The time will come—may it be very slow in its advance—when the gathering stars upon the pages of the Triennial will indicate that we are no longer an unbroken company. The coming years will find us left behind by one and another as they pass over the dark river, and the ties which bind us to old Yale will with our diminished numbers, themselves diminish—and it will be to the Children of the Class that we must look for the reminiscences of our college exploits, making them the chroniclers of our campaigns, the "Filles du Regiment" in our more peaceful army.

I trust and confidently expect to see at no distant day some of our number occupying with credit and honor the seats of instruction, and the professoral chairs in the halls of our Alma Mater. I am certain, sir, that they will look with peculiar interest at the annual ranks of "young gentlemen about to enter College," to see if the "sons of '56" shine out among them.

It is to be hoped that in such event the reminiscences of our doings here, which may then be still among old college legends, will be such only as to incite our representatives to industry and honesty—that the young —— may be reminded of the day when his father "*rushed,*" (when was it?) and not of his achievements in collecting the "Lamp Tax" and purloining Catalogues,—that Professor Paine, or Calkins, or Wilcox will remember to forget that the father of this young gentleman ever "argued the point," or that the parent of that one ever played Bacchanalian melodies as interludes at evening prayers; or that the distinguished gentleman who has just intrusted his son to their tutelage ever forgot himself so far as to mimic and "take off" a beloved professor.

To be sure, this is "taking a long look ahead." Before that time can come, friend D. must travel many a weary mile, in slight apparel, through the darkness, striving to find the "*stop*" to the small "*chamber organ*" which disturbs his slumbers! tempted perhaps to apply the "*Sub Bass*," but compelled to content himself with "*Haut boy*"—"Haut boy"!! Many a time and oft must B. and K. and T. rings the changes on Measles and Mumps, Croup, Chicken Pox and Worms, before the young bearers of their names will emulate the paternal deeds and win for themselves the degree of esteem and respect which their fathers enjoyed before them.

But although distant, I am conscious that the years are flying faster than of old, and I trust that I shall live to see the time which I have spoken of ; but whether so or not, I trust that when that day does come, our sons may find Old Yale, God bless her! as we have found her, a bountiful and cherishing mother, not only with larger stores of wealth, and rejoicing in her multiplied treasures of learning, and literary and scientific culture, but also with maternal and still increasing pride, regarding as her choicest jewels the long procession of her sons, and of these, ourselves not last or least remembered. That we may be able to reflect upon our Alma Mater some portion of the honor which her name has given us, is dependent in no mean degree upon the "wives of the class!"

I ought not to take my seat, without saying a single word respecting the especial ladies complimented in our sentiment—and yet I known not what that word should be. "The Wives of the Class." I respectfully submit, Sir, that a Bachelor has no right to "handle" that subject. What need of eulogy for them ? Their choice of partners from the class of '56 sufficiently approves their taste. The fact that they have themselves been chosen, establishes their excellence. I have not the pleasure of an acquaintance with any of them, but I hope that at our next re-union we shall see them present among us, and that "by their fruits we shall know them." After all, Sir, I apprehend that we Bachelors must confess that the perfect symmetry of life is only found where woman adds her complement, and that however much we may vaunt ourselves upon our single felicity, we yet inwardly agree with the language of the poet—was it Goldsmith or Pope ?—

> " Oh, Woman ! in our hours of ease,
> Uncertain, coy and hard to please,—"
> " But—seen too oft, familiar with thy face,
> We first endure, then pity, then embrace."

4

Let us, then, drink this sentiment in bumpers, invoking for all the " Wives of the Class," " *remque, prolemque et decus omne.*"

Then we sang the following song, written by C. T. CATLIN :

*AIR*—"*A little more Cider.*"

Come fellows, all, your voices raise
To swell the joyous strain ;
Hurrah, my boys, for " Fifty-Six,"
Hurrah, we meet again !
Then sing away, my jolly boys,
Till College wall and tower
Shall echo back the jovial song,
That tells the welcome hour !

*Chorus*—Oh, Hurrah, for " Fifty Six !"
Hurrah, for " Fifty-Six !"
Ring out the strain and shout again
Hurrah, for "Fifty-Six !"

Come Parsons, Doctors, Pedagogues,
And you, ye Legal crew,
Forget your sermons, books and fees,
And swell the chorus too !
You Business men to-night forego
Your money-making tricks,
To-night we're College boys, you know,
To-night we're "Fifty-Six !,'

*Chorus*—Oh, Hurrah, for " Fifty-Six !" &c.

Hurrah, my boys, we'll sing the praise
Of Alma Mater dear,
We'll sing the good old times we had
When we were students here !
We'll sing of Foot-ball, " Pow-wow," too,
Of Fresh Initiation,
Of " Jubilee," and " Wooden Spoon,"
And jolly Presentation !

*Chorus*—Oh, Hurrah, for "Fifty-Six !" &c.

Ah, fellows, yes, our hearts confess,
Where'er we chance to roam
We find no place like Alma Yale
Our dear old College *Home!*
Then sing away, my jolly bricks
And make a joyful noise,
To-night, to-night we're " Fifty-Six,"
To-night we're College boys !

*Chorus*—Oh, Hurrah, for " Fifty-Six !"

The next toast, "The Professions," was responded to by J. M. Brown, as follows :

Mr. President.—I regret that I should have been designated, at a late hour this evening, to respond to this toast. In the unavoidable failure of the gentleman at first selected, and whose serious indisposition is the apology for my appearance, the class have sustained a disappointment which ought to have been relieved by the substitution of some one whose abilities might warrant the compliment.

Among that large portion of the class who are exploring the intricacies of Theology, Law and Medicine, some one might surely have been found, the horizon of whose experience stretches beyond the humble bounds of a Police Court-room, and who has drawn inspiration from some more classic fount. And if the Secretary's book do not mislead us, *one* at least might have discoursed with equal versatility and profundity on the dangers and difficulties that hover around the Lawyer, the Teacher, the Physician, the Theologian and the Tutor.

If, sir, I am at a loss whether to laud the legal profession at the risk of offending the theologians, or to praise theology at the expense of my loyalty to the law, incurring in either case the professional censure of my medical classmates, the hesitation will not, I imagine, appear strange. It is not given to every one to blend the bitter pills of the three into a perfect sweet.

But perhaps as we were so closely knit together, while students, by our class ties and associations, and so united in sympathies and affection during the past three years, when separated and scattered, we may yet preserve a common purpose which will make us fellow-students still, and bind only stronger the unbroken chain that links us as friends and classmates. Though we pursue different roads, we are aiming at the same destination, our hopes high and our pulses throbbing with the same ambition as when we worked together over disputes in the division room, or fought the mimic fight in the arena of Linonia or the Brothers.

The aims of our class, how diverse and yet how similar—the character of the class, made up of how many elements and yet how it is mirrored in each individual—and our class peculiarities, how they are stamped upon each man of us as if thereby we should recognize one who belonged to Fifty-Six. And of these characteristics, some of mind, some of sentiment, some appealing to the poet, some to the utilitarian, there is one which will prove as valuable to us as professional men, as it was to us when students. It peculiarly belonged to our class while in College, and exhibited itself in an elasticity of temperament that dulls half the force of the buffets and disappointments that fate may have in store for us. Even after an unlooked-for depression, the inevitable working of this admirable faculty, on the principle that " Action and reaction are equal and in contrary directions," will be that the victim of one hour will become the hero of the next, and rebound, Antæus-like, into the regions of tranquility and content. Nor is it to be subdued by threats or forebodings, nor scared by the witty Saxe's lines, though he speaks with the air of one who has known what are the realizations of College hopes—

> " Alas for young ambition's vow,
>     How envious fate may overthrow it !
>     Poor Harvey is in Congress now,
>     Who struggled long to be a poet;
>     Smith carves (quite well) memorial stones,
>     Who tried in vain to make the law go;
>     Hall deals in hides, and " Pious Jones"
>     Is dealing faro in Chicago."

Even in the midst of calamities like these, must our philosophy shine forth, and decorate the misfortune with dignity   Our Congressman will adorn the national capital with all that grace that befits a president of Linonia or the Brothers.  Our carver of memorial tablets will rise superior to his fate and shine a conspicuous light in Geology or the respected proprietor of a marble quarry.  Our dealer in hides will (as one of our number has offered to do) furnish sheepskins for less than the faculty's fee; and if any of us should perchance " deal faro in Chicago," certainly in his hands the game will rise to the rank and dignity of a mathematical inquiry into the theory of chances.

Already our professional march has begun.  One of our number is clerk of a Police Court and leads our legal throng of forty young Blackstones.  Two of us are catalogued in the Triennial in that peculiar type that denotes the settled clergyman.  South Africa has renounced cannibalism and welcomed Robbins.  China, Germany, Greece and South America are familiar to some of us.

But the present condition of the class, and its history since graduation, belong to the Secretary's report, neither does it belong to me to narrate the memories of our College course.  It would be hard indeed to recall one by one all the incidents that make the memory linger about those happy years.  Only when the fog that collects each day between us and them, is dissipated by the sunshine of classmates' faces, and the memory quickened by an occasion like this, can we have an unclouded view of those beautiful isles that adorn the stream of our past career, and wish that the undiscovered lands of our future may be like them.

Sir, the happy past may be an earnest of our future. Those green spots that we think so fondly of, adorned with the temples of friendship, and perfumed with the fragrance of honest and manly hearts, were not the less securely based on the solid foundations of merit and intellect. Their loveliness did not surpass their worth, though the beauty of the vision now most attracts us. It is the union of intellect with heart that makes the recollection dear to us and invests each incident, as we recall it, with a rosy hue. The intellects that we respected in each other have been sharpened by contact with the world and whetted for the strife that awaits us; but in the hearty grasp of every classmate's hand to-night and the moistened eye that speaks sincerest joy, are the proofs that three years have not chilled that warmth of heart that made us love each as students, nor effaced those memories of Fifty-Six that are the omens of success for our class.

## We then sang Lauriger Horatius :

*Lauriger.*

Lauriger Horatius
  Quam dixisti verum,
Fugit Euro citius,
  Tempus edax rerum.
        *Chorus*—Ubi sunt O pocula,
                Dulciora melle,
                Rixæ, pax et oscula,
                Rubentis puellæ ?

Quid juvat æternitas
  Nominis, amare
Nisi terræ filias
  Licet, et potare!—*Chorus.*

Crescit uva molliter,
  Et puella crescit,
Sed poeta turpiter,
  Sitiens canescit.—*Chorus.*

Salve! Quinquaginta sex,
  Hodie beata!
Vale! Monitorum lex
  Nobis tam ingrata!

        *Chorus*—Ubi sunt O pocula,
                Dulciora melle,
                Rixæ, pax et oscula,
                Rubentis puellæ !

The fifth toast, " The Class of '56,—its future," was
responded to by L. L. PAINE, as follows :

MY CLASSMATES.—I have always thought that the powers of man
are never so severely tried, or so completely foiled, as when they
attempt to express, in words, the feelings of the heart,—those name-
less yearnings and throbbings, rich in unspeakable joy and thanksgiv-
ing, which cry for utterance in the hour of the soul's fullest, highest
life, but find no language. *Speech* is the natural servitor of intellect
or of passion; but the *emotion*, subtle in its processes as light, well-
ing up with resistless power from the very centre of our being, it has
no speech, no name. Thus it often happens that many words and
demonstrations, so far from showing emotion, show the want of it. The
truest miracle of feeling sometimes is a sublime silence. And so I
never rise to speak on an occasion like this, without feeling how utterly
impotent will be all the words which I can find, to image even in
faintest colors, the visions which play within and around me. And
especially *to-night*, do I envy those still, thoughtful spirits here, whose
happier lot it is, to yield themselves passively to the hallowing, hal-
lowed influences of this festive hour, and hold silent, secret converse
with faithful Memory and golden Hope.

Yes, brothers, no one has come here unattended to-night, to join in
our grand festival. Each one has come with a double escort—*Memory*,
laden with a thousand glad recollections, tinged, some few of them
perhaps, but oh how few! with a shade of sadness, and *Hope*, built
stoutly on a thousand aspirations, above which flit, like guardian moni-
tors, a thousand fears. Yes, *joyful* may we indeed be to-night, for no
requiem of misfortune or decay is to mingle with our glad songs;
*thankful* may we be, for no sad obituary will tell us that our circle is
broken; *hopeful* may we be, for I know that I but repeat the story of
your flashing eyes, and the prophecy of your beating hearts, when I
say that there has gathered here to-night, a band of *earnest men*. Am
I not right? Has a three years' trial and experience left no impress
on us? Are we not maturer, stronger, more practically earnest? Have
we not a clearer conception of our duty, a deeper interest in our des-
tiny? Yes, we have all of us, sensibly or insensibly, changed since
last we met on yonder green to say "farewell." Doubtless it has
been a matter of interest to you all, as it has to me, to scrutinize each
other's faces as you met, and there detect the half concealed trembling
lines, cunningly sketched by Time's kindliest hand,—lines yet to
deepen and widen into steep, unyielding furrows. And so these three

years have also been graving on our hearts, lines of habit and thought and conduct, which shall yet deepen and harden into firmest character. And in this fact we find a law, a key which, rightly used, may become a gift of prophecy. I know we may not boldly attempt to "forecast the years," but this we also know, that the Divine promise that seed time and harvest shall not fail, is but the special type of an eternal law. And in view of that law, what word of hopeful augury may I dare to utter for *the future* of our class ! My Classmates, I think I know you well. Four years of College life, affording peculiar opportunities for acquaintance, intimate and constant, such as often developed a rare and thorough knowledge of individual character, and sometimes ripened into holiest friendship,—four years of such intercourse and communion have not passed by without giving to each the criteria for judging of all. And as I know you, I will not, I *cannot* prophecy for the class of '56 a weary chase after honor and applause, eager only for a splendid triumph, careless of the right and the good, *for that has not been your character.* If any thing peculiarly distinguished the class of '56 in College, it was a quiet but sincere earnestness, which when deeply stirred rose to high enthusiasm and culminated in stubborn resolve. In this characteristic I place my confidence. For hath not earnestness within itself the seeds of *Duty ?* And is not Duty the germ of that true sense of *mission* which, rescuing the soul from the slavery of selfishness, grows all embracing in its charities, and flowers toward Heaven at last in self-forgetting sacrifice ?

And therefore catching a kind of divine afflatus from this inspiring presence, may I not predict for '56 a future of *noblest deeds* ! Beyond this I may not go ; for who would dare to unfold the mysteries which now lie buried in that " silent land "—that land yet unmarked by a single human footstep, where neither care nor woe, nor love nor joy hath entered, but where in supreme silence there reigns, we may believe and devoutly trust, the eternal will of a benignant Heavenly Father.

While then, with merry hearts and vocal jubilee we celebrate this, our glad reunion ; while we sing the songs that we used to sing, and hear the voices that we used to hear ; while memory leads us through her halls and wakes the sleepers there, and Hope beckons us winningly to follow her trusty guidance, let us, as earnest men, looking forward to the solemn issues of life, with heart and hand accept the sentiment which I now offer.

*The class of '56,—waiting,—watching for the post of duty.*

Then was sung the following song, written by C. T. CATLIN :

*AIR—" Shool."*

Come, Classmates, raise a hearty cheer,
Tell all the people far and near,
Old " Fifty-six" again is here !
Dis cum bibbalolla boo, slow reel !

    Shool, shool, shool I rool ;
    Shool I shack-a-rack, shool a barba cool :
    The first time I saw Silly bally e'el,
    Dis cum bibbalolla boo, slow reel !

Oh, swift the years have flown away
Since Prex dismissed us with " B. A.,"
And " Fifty-six" returns to-day !
Dis cum, &c.

We come our boyhood to renew,
Again the good old scenes to view
Where Profs and Tutors *put us through!*
Dis cum, &c.

Oh, ever since we came to town,
Old *Pond* of " pop" and " pie" renown,
*Has chased our fellows up and down ! !*
Dis cum, &c.

Ah, Pond, you're up to all the tricks—
No *hiding place* for " Fifty-six !"
Plague take your everlasting " *ticks !*"
Dis cum, &c.

Oh, where are all the Damsels fair,
Who came to *Lectures* from York Square ?
Egad, I wonder where they are !
Dis cum, &c.

And where are all the Syrens sweet,
We College fellows used to meet,
Whene'er we walked in Chapel street,
Dis cum, &c.

Alas, the girls whom you and I
Oft ogled with a tender sigh,
Have given place to *smaller fry !*
Dis cum, &c.

But come, my boys, a bumper mix,
And true to good old College " tricks,"
We drink " *The Girls of ' Fifty-six!*"
Dis cum, &c.

Now once again the chorus raise,
Sing out in Alma Mater's praise—
Hurrah, hurrah for College days!
Dis cum, &c.

The next toast, " Our Non-Graduate Members," was responded to by C. NORTHROP and G. B. BACON. All rose and in silence drank to the " Health of Absent Classmates." After this the roll was called, and each gave an account of his three years' experience ; some gave many amusing reminiscences of their college or subsequent life, and some told us their hopes for the future. The Secretary tried to record some of the good things that were said, but he found that while he was laughing at one joke, he forgot to set it down, or else lost the next, and therefore soon gave up the attempt in despair. The meeting was remarkable for the deep feeling and mutual confidence which prevaded it, and to which every one seemed impelled to give characteristic expression. Each felt that around him, at least, were sixty firm friends, who would ever rejoice in his success, and sympathize in his sorrows.—Thus eight hours of unalloyed happiness glided quickly away, and long before we were ready for it daylight admonished us to depart. Resolutions of thanks were accordingly passed, to the President of the meeting, to the Secretary, and to our Host, Mr. Allis. A resolution was passed, that the next general meeting should be held at the end of three years. We then proceeded to the Class Vine, and standing in a circle, we sang the parting song, written by G. B. BACON,

*AIR—"Auld Lang Syne."*

Oh sad and sweet the thoughts that throng
  Within our hearts to night ;
That mingle with our parting song
  As dawns the morning light.
Sweet thoughts of happy college years—
  Mem'ries that cannot die ;
Sad thoughts,—too strong and deep for tears—
  That stifle our "good-bye."

Sweet thoughts of days that rolled along,
  With brighter hopes and joys ;
Sweet thoughts of days we spent among
  These elms as college boys.
Sad thoughts that, boys no longer now,
  We deal with life's stern cares ;
Sad thoughts that soon on every brow,
  Shall glisten silver hairs.

Sad thoughts that we, who, gathered here,
  Raise high this choral strain,
Must part—at best, for many a year—
  And may not meet again.
Ah well ! as month by month shall wane—
  As passing years shall fade,
Till some of us come back again,
  After our first decade,—

So wane the months, so fade the years,
  Where'er our lot may fall,—
That brighter joys and lighter cares
  May be the lot of all.
But while we stand a lingering band,
  The winged moments fail;
We clasp each classmate's parting hand,
  And sing "GOD SAVE OLD YALE."

Then we shook hands all round, and having moved to the steps of the Lyceum, we gave nine cheers for '56, and as many more for Old Yale, and parted, happier and better men for the meeting.

# STATISTICS

# GRADUATED MEMBERS OF THE CLASS OF 1856.

---

### MATTHIAS HOLLENBACK ARNOT.

| | |
|---|---|
| Born at Elmira, New York, | Nov. 10, 1833 |
| Connected with the Class of '55, Yale, | |
| Entered Freshman, from Elmira, | Sept. 14, 1852 |

Engaged since graduation in business in Elmira,
chiefly superintending Gas works.
Expects to continue there.

### GILBERT FIELD BAILEY.

| | |
|---|---|
| Born at North Salem, New York, | Oct. 12, 1833. |
| Entered Freshman, from North Salem, | Sept. 15, 1852. |

Since graduating has been engaged in farming at
Croton Falls, New York.

| | |
|---|---|
| Married to Miss Georgia Pierce, of Dundee, N. Y. | May 18, 1859 |

### ROBERT MILTON BAKER.

| | |
|---|---|
| Born at Winchester, Va., | June 16, 1834. |
| Entered Sophomore, from Winchester, | Sept. 14, 1853. |

Studying Theology at Alexandria, Va.
Intends to be an Episcopal Clergyman.

### BENJAMIN FRANKLIN BARKER.

| | |
|---|---|
| Born at Berkshire, New York, | May 10, 1829. |
| Entered Junior, from Onondaga Valley, N. Y., | Sept. 20, 1854. |
| Principal of Onondaga Valley Academy, | 1856–57. |
| Studying Theology at home till | April 20, 1859, |

When he joined the conference of the M. Episcopal
Church and was stationed at Georgetown, Madison County, N. Y.

### GEORGE PAYSON BARKER.

| | |
|---|---|
| Born at Norwich, Conn., | Dec. 28, 1836. |
| Entered Freshman, from Norwich, Conn., | July 26, 1852. |
| Studying Law at Buffalo, N. Y. | |
| Admitted to the Bar, | Sept. 1859. |

### ANDREW JACKSON BARTHOLOMEW.

| | |
|---|---|
| Born at Hardwick, Mass., | Oct. 1, 1833. |
| Entered Freshman, from Hardwick, Mass., | July 27, 1852. |
| Studied Law in the office of Rice & Mason, at Worcester, | 1856–57. |
| At Cambridge Law School, | 1857–58. |
| Admitted to the Bar, | Feb. 1, 1858. |
| Began to practice at Southbridge, Mass., | Nov. 1858. |

### NELSON BARTHOLOMEW.

| | |
|---|---|
| Born at Hardwick, Mass., | Dec. 29, 1834. |
| Entered Freshman, from Hardwick, Mass., | July 27, 1852. |
| Studied Law in the office of Chas. Brimblecom, Esq., at Barre, Mass., | 1856–57. |
| In Cambridge Law School, | Sept. 1857—June 1858. |
| Admitted to the Bar, | Jan. 22, 1858. |
| Commenced practice at Oxford, Mass., | July 7, 1858. |
| Appointed Justice of the Peace, | Aug. 3, 1858. |

### ROBERT LINDSEY BRANDON.

| | |
|---|---|
| Born in Wilkinson Co. Miss., | Oct. 19 1835. |
| Entered Freshman, from Wilkinson Co., Miss. | Sept. 14, 1852. |
| Studying Engineering in New Haven, | 1856–57. |
| Since then, Planting. | |
| Post Office address, Fort Adams, Wilkinson Co. Miss. | |

### DAVID JOSIAH BREWER.

| | |
|---|---|
| Born at Smyrna, Asia Minor, | June 20, 1837. |
| Connected with Wesleyan University. | |
| Entered Junior, from Middletown, Conn. | Sept. 13, 1854. |
| In the office of David D. Field, Esq., N. Y. | 1856–57. |
| In Albany Law School, | 1857–58. |
| Admitted to the Bar of N. Y., in the Spring of | 1858. |
| At home "practicing on real estate" (with a hoe,) till Fall of | 1858. |
| When he went west and settled at Kansas City, Mo., till Spring of | 1859. |

Went to Pike's Peak and stayed two weeks.
Will probably settle at Lawrence or Leavenworth, Kansas.

### HORATIO NELSON BROCKWAY.

| | |
|---|---|
| Born at Lyme, Conn., | Nov. 8, 1834. |
| Entered Freshman, from Lyme, Conn., | Sept. 15, 1852. |

Is said to have been in Kansas.

### HENRY BILLINGS BROWN.

| | |
|---|---|
| Born in Berkshire Co., Mass., | March 2, 1836. |
| Entered Freshman, from Ellington, Conn., | July 27, 1852. |
| Traveled in Europe, | Oct. '56—Nov. 1857. |
| Studied Law in Ellington, with Hon. J. H. Brockway, | Dec. '57—Sept. 1858. |
| In Yale Law School, | Sept. '58—April 1859, |

When he joined Harvard Law School, where he
remains.
Post Office address, Mystic, Conn.

### JOHN MASON BROWN.

| | |
|---|---|
| Born at Frankfort, Ky., | April 26, 1837. |
| Entered Junior, from Frankfort, Ky., | Sept, 13, 1854. |
| Taught school in Frankfort, | '57—Spring of 1858. |
| In the Spring of 1858, Engineer in the State Geological survey till | July, 1858. |

Since then has been studying Law.

| | |
|---|---|
| Admitted to the Bar, | July 13, 1859. |

### THERON BROWN.

| | |
|---|---|
| Born at Westford, Conn., | April 29, 1832. |
| Entered Sophomore, from Westford, Conn., | Sept. 19, 1853. |
| In East Windsor Theological Seminary, | 1856–58. |
| In Newton Centre, (Mass.,) Theological Seminary, | 1858–59. |
| Licensed to preach, in the Fall of | 1856. |

### GEORGE WOLF BUEHLER.

| | |
|---|---|
| Born at Harrisburg, Pa., | Nov. 26, 1834. |
| Entered Freshman, from Harrisburg, Pa., | Sept. 14, 1852. |
| In the office of Civil and Mining Engineers, during the Winter | 1856–57. |
| Edited a paper for a friend in Harrisburg, | 1858. |
| Commenced editing and publishing the Farmers' and Miners' Journal, at Lykens, Pa., | Sept. 1858. |

### CHARLES EDWIN BULKELEY.

Born at Hartford, Conn.,                               Dec. 16, 1835.
Connected with Trinity College, class of                   1856.
Entered Junior, from Hartford,                      Sept. 13, 1854.
Since graduating has studied Law in his father's office.
Was admitted to the Bar,                            March, 1859.
Clerk of City Court, Hartford.

### WILLIAM ALDRICH BUSHEE.

Born at Worcester, Mass.,                            Jan. 31, 1833.
Entered Freshman, from Smithfield, R. I.,           Sept. 14, 1852.
Teaching in York Square Female Seminary, and
    studying in Yale Theological Seminary.              1856–59.

### PHINEAS WOLCOTT CALKINS.

Born at Corning, N. Y.,                             June 10, 1831.
Connected with the University of Rochester.
Entered Freshman, from Corning, N. Y.,              Oct. 7, 1852.
Taught at Wm. H. Russell's Institute, N. Haven, 1856—April, 1857.
Principal of the English Department of Wor-
    cester High School,            April, 1857—June 16, 1859.
Entered Union Theological Seminary,                 June, 1859.

### WILLIAM HENRY WILLSON CAMPBELL.

Born at Boston, Mass.,                              Oct. 23, 1833.
Entered Freshman, from Chelsea, Mass.,              July 28, 1852.
Edited a Fremont American Campaign paper in
    Waterbury, Conn., till after the election,             1856.
During the Winter was engaged in Mercantile
    studies in Boston.                                  1856–57.
Was teaching three months, during the Spring,
    at Washington, D. C.,                                1857.
Engaged as Meteorologist in the Atrato expe-
    dition, which was sent out for the verification
    of certain surveys for an interoceanic ship
    canal, near the Isthmus of Darien,      Oct. 1857—May, 1858.
Engaged in working up the results of the sur-
    vey at Washington, till April,                       1859.
Has been in Mercantile business in Boston ever since.
Address, No. 7 Wilson Lane, Boston, Mass.

### CHARLES TAYLOR CATLIN.

Born at New Brighton, Staten Island,               May 25, 1835.

Entered Freshman, from Brooklyn, Long Island,     July 26, 1852.
Teaching,                                               1857–58.
Has been residing in Brooklyn since graduation.
Expects soon to engage in financial operations.
Address, to the care of C. T. Catlin, Esq., N. Y. City.

### JOHN DENISON CHAMPLIN.

Born at Lexington, Ky.                           Jan. 29, 1834.
Entered Freshman, from Lexington, Ky.            July 26, 1852.
Studied Law with Gideon H. Hollister, Esq.,
    Litchfield, Conn.,
Admitted to the Bar,                               April, 1859.
Practicing Law at Milwaukie, Wis.

### ISAAC CLARK.

Born at South Coventry, Conn.                    June 30, 1833.
Entered Freshman, from South Coventry, Conn.     Sept. 15, 1852.
Teaching in Ellington, Conn.            Sept. 1856—July 1858.
Union Theological Seminary,                  1858—May 1859.
Since in Ellington, engaged in teaching.
Now in Andover Theological Seminary.

### ALFRED COIT.

Born at New London, Conn.                        May 23, 1835.
Entered Freshman, from New London,               July 26, 1852.
Studied Law nine months with Robert Coit, Jr.,
    Esq., New London.
In Yale Law School,                        May—Sept. 1857.
Harvard Law School,                             1857–58.
Received L. L. B., at Harvard,                      1858.
Admitted to the Bar at New London,             Nov. 1858.
Practicing in New London.

### STEPHEN CONDIT.

Born at Orange, N. J.                            Sept. 23, 1835.
Entered Freshman, from Orange, N. J.             July 26, 1852.
In the Law office of Gov. Pennington, Newark, N. J.    1856–57.
Yale Law School,                                1857–58.
Admitted to the Bar in Poughkeepsie, N. Y.       May, 1859.
In partnership with his brother in Brooklyn, L. Island.

### EDWARD ORSON COWLES.

Born at Woodstock, Conn.                         Dec. 22, 1834.

Entered Freshman, from North Haven, Conn.          July 26, 1852.
Teaching in Trumansburg, N. Y.                        1856–57.
Managing his father's farm in Summer of                 1859.
Now studying Medicine in New Haven.

### JAMES OTIS DENNISTON.

Born at Salisbury Mills, N. Y.                     Dec. 14, 1835.
Entered Freshman, from Salisbury Mills, N. Y.      July 27, 1852.
Studied Law with E. A. Brewster, Esq., New-
    burg, N. Y. '                                  1856–58.
And was then admitted to practice.
Practicing in the office of Hall, Vanderpool &
    Co. 237 Broadway, N. Y., from                 Oct. 1858.
Now practicing at 61 Wall street, N. Y.

### CHAUNCEY MITCHELL DEPEW.

Born at Peekskill, N. Y.                          April 23, 1834.
Entered Freshman, from Peekskill, N. Y.           July 30, 1852.
Stumped for Fremont three months.
Studied Law at Peekskill,                             1856–58.
Admitted to the Bar,                               March, 1858.
Sent as delegate to the Republican State Conven-
    tion for the third district of Westchester Co.   Sept. 8, 1858.
Practicing Law at Peekskill, "beautifully situa-
    ted on the banks of the Hudson."

### ARTHUR DICKINSON.

Born at Macon, Ga.                                  July, 1835.
Entered Sophomore, from Macon, Ga.                 Oct. 1, 1853.
Studied Law at Macon, Ga.                             1856–58.
Admitted to the Bar, and practicing in Macon, Ga.
Married to Miss Margaret Town of Macon, Ga,        Aug. 1858.

### GEORGE MORRIS DORRANCE.

Born at Bristol, Pa.                               Sept. 6, 1836.
Connected with the College of New Jersey.
Entered Junior, from Bristol, Pa.                 Sept. 15, 1854.
At home,                                             1856–58.
Entered the Law office of Benj. H. Brewster,
    Esq., Philadelphia.                           Dec. 28, 1858.

### VIRGIL MARO DOW.

| | |
|---|---|
| Born at New Haven, Conn. | April 5, 1833. |
| Connected with the class of 1855, Yale, | |
| Entered Sophomore, from New Haven, | Sept. 30, 1853. |
| Studied Medicine, | 1856–57. |
| In the perfumery business, New York, | 1857–58. |
| Apothecary in New Haven since | July 1858. |

### HASBROUCK DU BOIS.

| | |
|---|---|
| Born at Fishkill, N. Y. | Nov. 27, 1833. |
| Entered Freshman, from Fishkill, N. Y. | July 26, 1852. |
| Studied Theology at New Brunswick, N. J. | 1856—June 1859. |
| Settled over the North Dutch Church Newark, N. J. | June 1, 1859. |

### ROBERT CHOTARD DUNBAR.

| | |
|---|---|
| Born at Natchez, Miss. | Sept. 16, 1834. |
| Entered Freshman, from Natchez, Miss., | Sept. 14, 1852. |
| Since graduating has been engaged in Planting near Natchez. | |

### GEORGE CARY DUNHAM.

| | |
|---|---|
| Born at Pittsfield, Mass. | Oct. 11, 1832. |
| Entered Freshman, from Pittsfield, Mass. | Sept. 14, 1852. |
| Teaching and practicing Music in Pittsfield, Mass., since graduating. | |
| Married to Miss Melissa Smith, of Fair Haven, Conn. | Oct. 19, 1857. |
| A son born, | June 17, 1858. |
| A daughter born, | June 27, 1859. |

### IRA DUNLAP.

| | |
|---|---|
| Born at Middleport, N. Y. | Feb. 22, 1832. |
| Entered Freshman, from Middleport, N. Y. | Sept. 30, 1852. |
| Traveling and settling his father's estate, | 1856–57. |
| Engaged in Banking at Rochester, Fall of | 1857. |
| Expects to continue there. | |

### EMMET ALEXANDER EAKIN.

| | |
|---|---|
| Born in Bedford County, Tenn. | March 26, 1836. |
| Entered Freshman, from Nashville, Tenn. | July 26, 1852. |
| Engaged in farming in Fall of | 1857. |
| Married to Miss Jane Ewing of Nashville, | Dec. 3, 1856. |
| Daughter, Rowena Eakin, born | Dec. 3, 1857. |
| Post office address, Jefferson, Tenn. | |

6

### CHARLES EDWARD FELLOWES.

| | |
|---|---|
| Born at Hartford, Conn. | June 17, 1834. |
| Entered Freshman, from Hartford, Conn. | July 26, 1852. |

Teaching most of the time at Bloomfield, N. J.  July 1856—Oct. '58.
Afterwards studying Law in his father's office,
   and admitted to the Bar,                   July 26, 1859.

### FRANK FELLOWES.

Born at Hartford, Conn.                       May 8, 1830.
Connected with class of '54, Yale.
Entered Junior, from Hartford,              Oct. 1854.
Since graduating has studied Law in his father's office.
Admitted to the Bar,                March 26, 1859.
Intends to practice in Hartford.

### LUKE WILLIAM FINLAY.

Born at Oak Grove, near Brandon, Miss.      Oct. 8, 1831.
Connected with Brandon College, Miss.
Entered Sophomore, from Brandon, Miss.     Oct. 17, 1853.
Had charge of the Male Academy in Brandon,   1856–57.
Went to Memphis, Tenn.               Aug. 1, 1857.
Licensed to practice Law,           March 9, 1858.
Taught select School at Memphis, Tenn., two
   and a half months.
Entered Chancery office as deputy clerk and
   Master in Chancery              Aug. 16, 1858.
Expects to practice as Attorney at Memphis.

### LOUIS CHRISTOPHER FISCHER.

Born at Baltimore, Md.               Aug. 3, 1834.
Entered Sophomore, from Baltimore, Md.   Sept. 14, 1853.
During the first two years had no settled occupation.
In the third year commenced the study of Law.

### JOHN MINOT FISKE.

Born at Boston, Mass.               Aug. 17, 1834.
Entered Freshman, from Chelmsford, Mass.  Sept. 14, 1852.
In Law office of Rowe & Bartlett, Bangor, Me.  1856–57.
Harvard Law School,               1857–58.
Admitted to the Bar,              June, 1858.
In the office of Seth J. Thomas, Esq., during winter of  1858–59.
Practicing Law at 46 Court Street, Boston.

### JOSEPH RICHARDSON FRENCH.

Born at Andover, Mass. June 12, 1836.
Entered Freshman, from Andover, Mass. Sept. 14, 1852.
Teaching at Stockbridge and Abingdon, Mass. Aug. 1856—April '58.
Studying Law in Boston, April—Sept. 1858.
Studying Law in Andover, Sept. 1858—April 1859.
Where he at present remains.

### JULIUS GAY.

Born at Farmington, Conn. Feb. 15, 1834.
Entered Freshman, from Farmington, Conn. July 26, 1852.
In Yale Engineering School, 1856–58.
The past year in Farmington.

### THEODORE PARSONS HALL.

Born at Hartford, Conn. Dec. 15, 1835.
Entered Freshman, from Binghampton, N. Y. Sept. 14, 1852.
Studying Law at Binghampton, N. Y. 1856–57.
In the Banking House of John Thompson,
  Wall street, N. Y. 1857–59,
Became Cashier of the State Bank of Michigan,
  at Detroit, 1859.
Intends to continue Banking.

### ALEXIS WYNNS HARRIOTT.

Born on Turks Island, W. I. Sept. 24, 1835.
Entered Freshman, from Turks Island, July 26, 1853.
Since graduating has been studying at Yale Engi-
  neering School, except a few months spent in visi-
  ting the West Indies.
Received the degree of B. P., July 28, 1859.

### WILLIAM JAMES HARRIS.

Born at West Brattleboro, Vt. May, 1834.
Connected with Williams College, class of 1856.
Entered Junior, from West Brattleboro, Sept. 13, 1854.
Engaged in teaching at St. Stephens, New Bruns-
  wick, 1856 to Spring of 1859.
Principal of the Academy at Monson, Mass.
Married to Miss Mary G. Hill, of St. Stephens, N. B. Aug. 18, 1859.

### FRANK HODGE.

Born at Buffalo, N. Y. 1833.
Entered Sophomore, from Buffalo, N. Y. Sept. 26, 1853.

Since graduating has been studying Medicine, except a few months spent in the North West, on a hunting expedition.   Expects a diploma this Fall and to practice " Allopath, the straight and narrow path."

### FREDERICK STREET HOPPIN.

Born at Providence, R. I.,                                June 10, 1834.
Entered Freshman from Providence, R. I.,                  July 27, 1852.
Engaged in business in Providence,                          1856–57.
Since, studying law and admitted to the Bar this Summer.
Intend to practice in Providence.

### WILBUR JOHNSON.

Born at Genoa, New York,                                  March 1, 1831.
Entered Freshman, from New Haven, Conn.,                  July 14, 1852.
Teaching in Plymouth, Conn.,                           1856.—Dec. 1857.
Spending vacation in New Haven studying Surveying.
Teaching in Rochester, Mass.,                           57.—Dec. 1858.
Teaching in Collinsville, Conn.,                          1858–59.
Thinks he shall continue to teach.

### SENECA McNEIL KEELER.

Born at Ridgefield, Conn.,                                May 31, 1835.
Fntered Freshman, from Ridgefield,                        July 27, 1852.
Went to Natchez, Miss., as private tutor,                   1856.
Returned in a few months, declining a second engagement.
Engaged in teaching at North Salem, N. Y.,                 1856–58.
Engaged in teaching at Kingsboro, N. Y.,                 Fall of 1858.
Married to Miss Alice B. Smith, of N. Salem,             Aug. 24, 1857·
Daughter, Laura Frances, born,                            Oct. 2, 1858.
Now teaching an Academy at East Bloomfield,
    Ontario Co. New York,

### WYLLYS SEYMOUR KING.

Born at St. Louis, Mo.,                                   Dec. 15, 1834.
Entered Sophomore, from St. Louis, Mo.,                   Oct. 3, 1833.
Engaged in business with his father at St. Louis.

### ROLAND KINZER.

Born at Lancaster, Pa.,                                  March 17, 1835.
Entered Freshman, from Lancaster, Pa.,                    July 26, 1852.
Reading Law in the office of Thaddeus Stevens, M. C.        56–58.
· Admitted to the bar,                                    Jan. 1859.
Practicing Law at Lancaster.

### WILLIAM TILDEN KITTREDGE.

Born at Norwalk, Ohio, Sept. 21, 1835.
Entered Freshman, from Norwalk, Ohio, Sept. 14, 1852.
Studied Law in Cincinnati, and was admitted to the Bar, April, 1858.
Settled at Wilton, Waseca county, Minnesota, May, 1859.

### WILLIAM LAMSON.

Born at Keene, N. H., Dec. 22, 1834.
Entered Freshman, from Keene, N. H., July 27, 1852.
Since graduating has been engaged with his father in
the tanning business, and will furnish the class with
sheep skins at a discount.

### GROVE PETTIBONE LAWRENCE.

Born at Norfolk, Conn., Nov. 19, 1831.
Entered Freshman, from Norfolk, Conn., Oct. 4. 1852.
Since graduating has been engaged in farming.

### GUSTAVE ADOLPHE LEMEE.

Born at Natchitoches, La., Feb. 20, 1835.
Entered Freshman, from Natchitoches, La., Sept. 15, 1852.
Was engaged in teaching from Nov. 1, 1856 to Nov. 1857.
Attended Law lectures at the University in New
Orleans during the winter, 1857–8.
Admitted to the Bar, Aug. 1858.
Practicing Law in Nachitoches.

### HENRY MARTIN MᶜINTIRE.

Born near Elkton, Cecil Co. Md., March 19, 1835.
Entered Freshman, from Elkton, Md., Sept. 15, 1852.
Commenced to study Law with Hon. Jos. J. Lewis,
Westchester, Pa., Sept. 15, 1856.
Admitted to the Bar, Sept. 18, 1858.
Now practicing in Westchester, Pa.

### BENJAMIN DRAKE MAGRUDER.

Born at Baton Rouge, La., Sept. 27, 1838.
Entered Freshman, from Jackson, La., Sept. 14, 1852.
Studied Law in New Orleans, but was not admitted
to the Bar on account of "infancy."

### CHARLES MANN.

Born at Utica, New York, May 29, 1835.
Entered Freshman, from Utica, July 28, 1852.

In Europe,                                          Oct. 1856—Oct. 1857.
Studied Law in Utica, N. Y.,                        Oct. 1857—Dec. 1858.
And then in office of Mann & Rodman, N. Y. City.
Admitted to the Bar,                                          May, 1859.
Now practicing at 39 Wall Street, New York.

### JUSTIN MARTIN.

Born at Chaplin, Conn.,                             Feb. 7, 1834.
Entered Freshman, from Chaplin, Conn.,              Sept. 15, 1852.
Teaching in New York most of the time since graduation.

### LEWIS ESTE MILLS.

Born at Morristown, N. J.,                          Aug. 13, 1836.
Entered Freshman, from Morristown, N. J.,           Sept. 14, 1852.
Studied Law in the office of Miller & Mills, in
    Morristown,                                     1856—Oct. 1857.
Entered office of Mills & Hoadley, Cincinnati,      Nov. 1858.
Admitted to the Bar,                                Nov. 1858.
A member of the law firm of Mills & Hoadley.

### JOHN MONTEITH.

Born at Elyria, N. Y.,                              Jan. 31, 1833.
Connected with Western Reserve,
Entered Junior, from Elyria, N. Y.,                 Sept. 14, 1834.
Studied Theology in Yale Theological Sem. till May,          1858.
Then he was invited to Terryville, Conn. to preach,
    and was ordained and installed at that place,   Oct. 27, 1858.

### JOHN MOREHEAD.

Born at Frankfort, Ky.,                             March 4, 1837.
Entered Junior, from Frankfort, Ky.,                Sept. 13, 1854.
Since graduating, has studied Law at Frankfort.
Admitted to the Bar.
Intends to settle in Louisville.

### SIDNEY EDWARDS MORSE.

Born in New York City,                              Nov. 25, 1835.
Entered Freshman, from New York,                    July 26, 1852.
Sailed for Hong Kong,                               Aug. 4, 1856.
Arrived after a passage of 119 days. Visited Canton,
    Macao, &c.  Was detained at Hong Kong, by the
    Chinese disturbances, till                      Jan. 20, 1857.
Arrived home, via. San Francisco and Aspinwall, after
    an absence of 8 months.

Immediately entered the office of the N. Y. Observer,
And took the place of his father as partner, in the Summer,      1857.
Expects to continue there.

### EDWARD PAYSON NETTLETON.

Born at Sprinfield, Mass.,                                    Nov. 7, 1834.
Entered Freshman, from Chicopee, Mass.,                      July 27, 1852.
Spent three months in Illinois, sharpening and driv-
    ing grade pegs on a prairie railroad—getting tired
    of this, he cut sticks and went to Virginia, and
    taught school about 6 months.
Took charge of the Academy at Chicopee, Mass., till,      Dec. 1858.
In Law office of Gordon L. Ford, Esq., 23 Wall St., N. Y.,   1858–59.

### LEWIS RICHARD PACKARD.

Born at Philadelphia, Pa.,                                   Aug. 22, 1836.
Entered Freshman, from Philadelphia,                        July 26, 1852.
In New Haven,                                        Sept. 1856—Aug. 57.
In Europe, traveling and studying in University of
    Berlin,                                         Aug. 1857—Oct. 58.
At home studying Hebrew, with a view to the ministry,       1858–59.
Elected Tutor at Yale,                                      July, 1859.
Tutor in Freshman Mathematics.

### LEVI LEONARD PAINE.

Born at East Randolph, Mass.,                               Oct. 10, 1832.
Entered Freshman, from Randolph,                           Sept. 14, 1852.
Principal of Classical Department of Norwalk High
    School,                                                 1856–57.
Teaching Greek in Mr. Russell's Institute, N. H.,           1857–59.
In Yale Law School,                                         1857–58.
In Yale Theological Seminary,                               1858–59.
Elected Tutor in Yale College,                             July, 1858.
Now Tutor in Junior Greek.

### HENRY EDWARDS PARDEE.

Born at Trumbull, Conn.,                                    Aug. 11, 1831.
Entered Freshman, from Trumbull,                           Aug. 26, 1852.
Teaching in Mr. Russell's School, and Reading Law
    with H. B. Harrison, Esq.,                              1856–59.
In Yale Law School one term,                                1859.
Entered office of E. I. Sanford, Esq., New Haven,       Aug. 17, 1859.
Will be admitted to the Bar this fall,
                                                            1860

admitted March

### GEORGE ELEAZER HOLT PEASE.

Born at Norfolk, Conn.,                                   Aug. 31, 1833.
Entered Freshman, from Norfolk,                           Sept. 25, 1852.
Removed to Dayton, O., soon after graduating, and
    read Law in the office of Judge Holt.
Studied Law in the office of Judge Vandover, Spring-
    field, Ill.
Admitted to the Bar,                                     Nov. 1857.
Practicing at Pana, Christian Co., Ill.
Thrown from a carriage and had broken his leg, this Summer.
Now Mayor of the city.

### FRANK HENRY PECK.

Born at New Haven, Conn.,                                Sept. 20, 1836.
Entered Freshman, from New Haven, Conn.,                 July 26, 1852.
Principal of Academy, West Killingly, Conn.,                1856–57.
Clerk of Probate Court for New Haven District,           Aug. 1857.
Studied Law in Yale Law School,                            1857–59.
Elected Grand Juror,                                     Nov. 1858.
Admitted to the Bar,                                     May, 1859.
Practicing Law in New Haven.

### SAMUEL LYMAN PINNEO.

Born at Newark, N. J.,                                   Sept. 21, 1835.
Entered Freshman, from Newark, N. J.,                    July 27, 1852.
Traveling in the West two or three months; the
    rest of the year at home,                              1856—57.
In Union Theological Seminary,          Fall of 1857—June, 1858.
Sailed for Europe,                                      June, 1858.
Traveling in Europe, Egypt and the Holy Land,   1858—Aug. 1859.
Intends to continue his studies at Union Theo. Seminary.

### JOHN THOMAS PRICE.

Born at Arrow Rock, Mo.,                                 July 13, 1836.
Entered Freshman, from Arrow Rock, Mo.,                  July 27, 1852.
Now in Europe.

### JAMES LYMAN RACKLEFF.

Born at Portland, Me.,                                   Feb. 9, 1836.
Entered Freshman, from Bridgton, Me.,                    July 26, 1852.
Teaching as private tutor in Louisiana,                   1856—57.
In Yale Law School,                                       1857—58.
In the law office of E. I. Sanford, Esq. three months
    in the fall of                                         1858.
Private tutor in Louisiana during the Winter,             1858—59.

Admitted to the Bar at Chicago, Ill., in the Spring,     1859.
Practicing Law at El Paso, Woodford Co., Ill.

### DAVID PLUNKETT RICHARDSON.

Born at Macedon, N. Y.     May 28, 1833.
Entered Sophomore, from Macedon,     Sept. 14, 1853.
Teaching in Angelica, N. Y.     1856—April 1859.
Since then has been studying Law in the office of
    Rawson & Stebbins, Rochester, N. Y.

### CLARKE RIGHTER.

Born at Northeast, N. Y.     Nov. 20, 1833.
Entered Freshman, from Northeast,     Feb. 1, 1853.
Professor in Jefferson College, Miss.,     1856–57.
Private tutor in Washington, Miss.,     Feb.—Aug. 1857.
Studying Law in Lakeville, Conn.,     1857–59.

### ELIJAH ROBBINS.

Born at Thompson, Conn.,     March 12, 1828.
Entered Sophomore, from Westford, Conn.,     Sept. 14, 1853.
In East Windsor Theological Seminary,     1856–59.
Licensed to preach,     April 19, 1858.
Appointed Missionary of the A. B. C. F. M.,     Jan. 25, 1859.
Graduated,     July 21, 1859.
Ordained an Evangelist at E. Hartford,     Aug. 3, 1859.
Married to Miss Addie Bissell,     Aug. 17, 1859.
Sailed from Boston about the 5th of September, as
    Missionary to the Zulus, South Africa.

### GEORGE CHESTER ROBINSON.

Born at Wellsboro, Pa.,     Aug. 1833.
Connected with Genesee College.
Entered Freshman, from Wellsboro, Pa.,     May 3, 1853.
Studying Theology in New York,     1856—April 1858.
Joined the Conference of the Methodist E. Church,     April 1858.
Appointed to the First Place Church, Brooklyn,     1858–59.
Pastor of a Church in Cincinnati, O.,     April 1859.
Married to Miss Maria M. Stevens of New York,     Aug. 4, 1858.

### DONALD DOUGLAS SHAW.

Born at Hamden, N. Y.     June 22, 1835.
Entered Freshman, from Hamden, N. Y.,     Sept. 20, 1852.
At Albany Law School,     1856–57.
Now in Europe.

### EDWARD ALFRED SMITH.

| | |
|---|---|
| Born at West Woodstock, Conn., | July 22, 1835. |
| Entered Freshman, from New York City, | July 27, 1852. |
| In New Haven, pursuing general studies and Theology, | 1856–58. |
| Entered Andovor Theological Seminary in the Fall of | 1858. |

### CHARLES GOODRICH SOUTHMAYD.

| | |
|---|---|
| Born at New Orleans, La., | Oct. 18, 1834. |
| Entered Sophomore, from New Orleans, | July 26, 1853. |

Since graduating has been engaged with, and now is
head clerk of Neill Brothers & Co., Cotton Factors,
Union street, New Orleans, La.

### ANDREW JACKSON STEINMAN.

| | |
|---|---|
| Born at Lancaster, Pa., | Oct. 10, 1836. |
| Entered Freshman, from Lancaster, Pa., | Oct. 9, 1852. |
| In the Albany Law School during the Winter, | 1856–57. |
| Reading Law in Lancaster, | 1857–59. |

Admitted to the Bar at the August session, and intends to practice in Lancaster.

### JOHN BUFFINGTON STICKNEY.

| | |
|---|---|
| Born at Lynn, Mass., | May 25, 1832. |
| Entered Senior, from Lynn, Mass., | Sept. 1855. |

Admitted to the Bar of Mass.,

### JOHN WAGER SWAYNE.

| | |
|---|---|
| Born at Columbus, O., | Nov. 10, 1834. |

Connected with the Class of 1855, Yale.

| | |
|---|---|
| Entered Sophomore, from Columbus, O., | Sept. 15, 1853. |
| In the Law office of Swayne & Baber, Columbus, O. | 1856–58. |
| Entered Cincinnati Law School, | Oct. 1858. |

Expects, after graduating, to become a member of the
above named firm.

### CHARLES ALBERT SWIFT.

| | |
|---|---|
| Born at Warren, Conn. | June 29, 1837. |
| Entered Freshman, from Warren, Conn. | Sept. 14, 1852. |

Principal of the High School at Sacramento, Cal.

### OLIVER STARR TAYLOR.

| | |
|---|---|
| Born at Brookfield, Conn. | March 14, 1832. |
| Entered Freshman, from Brookfield, Conn. | Sept. 14, 1852. |
| In Yale Theological Seminary. | 1856–58. |

Preached three months in New Preston, five months
in Winsted, and since in Simsbury.
Married to Miss Lottie Baldwin, of Bridgeport, Conn.  July 6, 1858.

### EDWARD CORNELIUS TOWN.

| | |
|---|---|
| Born at Goshen, Mass. | Oct. 1834. |
| Connected with Beloit College. | |
| Entered Sophomore, from Batavia, Ill. | Feb. 11, 1854. |
| Studying Theology in New York, | 1856–57. |
| Continuing studies and teaching in New Haven. | 1857–59. |

### WILLIAM ELISHA TURNER.

| | |
|---|---|
| Born at Northampton, Mass. | Sept. 9, 1834. |
| Entered Freshman, from Northampton, Mass. | Sept. 15, 1852. |
| Studied Law in the office of Baker & Delano, | 1856–59. |
| Admitted to the Bar, | Feb. 3, 1859. |

Now in partnership with Chas. Delano, Esq.  Name of
the firm, Delano & Turner, Northampton, Mass.

### AUGUSTUS HALL WALKER.

| | |
|---|---|
| Born at Fryeburg, Me. | Dec, 22, 1833. |
| Entered Junior, from Fryeburg, Me. | Nov. 9, 1854. |
| Studying Law with Wm. P. Fessenden and M. B. | |
| Butler, Portland, Me. | 1856–58. |

After admission to the Bar, traveled in Minnesota,
with a view to location.
Now at home taking charge of a sick brother.

### EDWARD ASHLEY WALKER.

| | |
|---|---|
| Born at New Haven, Conn. | Nov. 24, 1834. |
| Entered Freshman, from New Haven, Conn. | July 26, 1852. |
| In Yale Theological Seminary, | 1856—Spring of 1858. |
| Preached at Terryville, Conn., three months in the Spring of | 1858. |
| Sailed for Europe, | Sept. 1858. |
| Studied at Heidelberg, | 1858–59. |

Intends to study a year at Berlin.

### BENJAMIN WEBB.

| | |
|---|---|
| Born in New York City, | Aug. 1831. |
| Entered Freshman, from New York City, | Aug. 23, 1852. |

Spent three months at a Water Cure.  Having been
cured of the " Cure," was private tutor in the family of John Murdock, Esq., at Rodney, Miss.  1856—June 1857.

Tutor in the family of Dandridge Gale, Esq., of
  Loretto, Va.                                    June to Nov. 1857.
Became Principal of Academy in North Green-
  wich, Conn.                                     May 24, 1859.

### JAMES LYMAN WHITNEY.

Born at Northampton, Mass.                         Nov. 28, 1835.
Entered Freshman, from Northampton,               July 27, 1852.
In New Haven as Berkeley scholar,                      1856–57.
In the Book publishing house of Wiley & Halsted, N. Y.  1857–58.
In the Book publishing house of Bridgeman & Co.
  Springfield, Mass.                                    1858–59.

### TIMOTHY KEELER WILCOX.

Born at North Greenwich, Conn.                    May 18, 1835.
Entered Freshman, from New Haven,                 July 26, 1852.
Teaching in Hartford High School,           1856—May 1859.
Entered Yale Theological Seminary,                  May 1859.
Elected Tutor at Yale,                             July 1858.
Now Tutor in Freshman Latin.

### AHAB GEORGE WILKINSON.

Born at Willimantic, Conn.                             1831.
Entered Freshman, from Willimantic,               July 28, 1852.
Has had charge of the Classical department of several
  Washington, D. C., Academies, and has been en-
  gaged in fitting private pupils for College.         1856–59.
Married to Miss Julia A. Dorman, of Enfield, Conn.  Aug. 20, 1857.
Had a daughter born, which lived only a short time,  May 12, 1859.
Mrs. Wilkinson died of Pneumonia,                 May 14, 1859.

### EDWARD FRANKLIN WILLIAMS.

Born at Uxbridge, Mass.                           July 22, 1832.
Entered Freshman, from Uxbridge,                 Sept. 14, 1852.
Teaching constantly since graduating, at Merwins-
  ville, Conn.                                         1856–59.
Now studying Theology at Princeton.

### JOHN DUNN WOOD.

Born in New York City,                            Oct. 5, 1837.
Entered Freshman, from New York City,           Sept. 15, 1852.

After graduating, was clerk in the E. India House of
his father, and sailed as agent for the firm, for Sin-
gapoor, East Indies,             Feb. 14, 1854.
Intends to remain there a number of years.

### SAMUEL FAY WOODS.

Born at Barre, Mass.             June 23, 1837.
Entered Freshman, from Barre,        July 27, 1852.
Studied law in the office of Bacon & Aldrich, Wor-
cester,           Sept. 1856—June 1857.
In Harvard Law School,      Sept. 1857—July 1858.
Admitted to the Bar,          Aug. 17, 1858.
Opened an office at Barre,        Sept. 10, 1858.

### HENRY EDGAR WOOTON.

Born at Rockville, Md.         Sept. 21, 1837.
Connected with Georgetown College.
Entered Junior, from Rockville,     Sept. 13, 1854.
Studied Law in Rockville,          1856–57.
Studied Law in Baltimore,         1856–59.
Expects to practice in Baltimore.

### JOHN HUNTER WORRALL.

Born in Delaware Co., Md.            1827.
Entered Freshman, from Montgomery Co., Pa.    July 26, 1852.
Principal of Westchester Academy,    Oct. 1, 1856—1859.
Intends to enter Scientific School at Yale in October next.

# SUMMARY

## OF THE

# STATISTICS OF GRADUATES.

### I. PLACE OF BIRTH.

*Connecticut.*—G. P. Barker, Brockway, T. Brown, Bulkeley, Clark, Coit, Cowles, Dow, F. Fellowes, C. Fellowes, Gay, Hall, Keeler, Lawrence, Martin, Pardee, Pease, Peck, Robbins, Smith, Swift, Taylor, E. A. Walker, Wilcox, Wilkinson.—25.

*New York.*—Arnot, Bailey, B. F. Barker, Calkins, Catlin, Denniston, Depew, DuBois, Dunlap, Hodge, Johnson, Mann, Morse, Richardson, Righter, Shaw, Webb, Wood.—18.

*Massachusetts.*—A. J. Bartholomew, N. Bartholomew, H. B. Brown, Bushee, Campbell, Dunham, Fiske, French, Nettleton, Paine, Stickney, Town, Turner, Whitney, Williams, Woods.—16.

*Pennsylvania.*—Buehler, Dorrance, Kinzer, Packard, Robinson, Steinman, Worrall.—7.

*New Jersey.*—Condit, Mills, Pinneo.—3.

*Ohio.*—Kittredge, Monteith, Swayne.—3.

*Maryland.*—Fischer, McIntire, Wootton.—3.

*Kentucky.*—J. M. Brown, Champlin, Morehead.—3.

*Louisiana.*—Lemée, Magruder, Southmayd.—3.

*Mississippi.*—Brandon, R. C. Dunbar, Finlay.—3.

*Maine.*—Rackleff, A. H. Walker.—2.

*Missouri.*—King, Price.—2.

*Vermont.*—Harris.—1.

*New Hampshire.*—Lamson.—1.

*Rhode Island.*—Hoppin.—1.

*Virginia.*—Baker.—1

*Georgia.*—Dickinson.—1.

*Tennessee.*—Eakin.—1.

*West Indies.*—Harriott.—1.

*Asia Minor.*—Brewer.—1.

### II. TIME OF BIRTH.

1827.—Worrall.—1.

1828.—Robbins.—1.

1829.—B. F. Barker.—1.

1830.—F. Fellowes.—1.

1831.—Johnson, Calkins, Webb, Pardee, Finlay, Lawrence.—6.

1832.—Dunlap, Taylor, T. Brown, Stickney, Williams, Paine, Dunham.—7.

1833.—Bushee and Monteith, Dow, Richardson, Clark, Robinson, Pease, A. J. Bartholomew, Bailey, Campbell, Arnot, Righter, DuBois, Hodge,* A. H. Walker.—15.

1834.—Champlin, Martin, Gay, Wilkinson, Depew, Harris, Hoppin, Baker, C. Fellowes, Fischer, Fiske, Turner, Dunbar, Town, Nettleton, Brockway, Swayne, E. A. Walker, King, Cowles and Lamson, N. Bartholomew, Southmayd*.—23.

1835.—Lemée, Kinzer, McIntire, Wilcox, Coit, Catlin, Mann, Keeler, Dickinson, Shaw, Smith, Kittredge and Pinneo, Condit, Harriott, Brandon, Whitney, Morse, Denniston, Hall, Bulkeley.—21

1836.—Rackleff, H. B. Brown, Eakin, French, Price, Mills, Packard, Dorrance, Peck, Steinman, Buehler, G. P. Barker.—12.

1837.—Morehead, J. M. Brown, Brewer, Woods, Swift, Wooton, Wood.—7.

1838.—Magruder.—"Heir of all the ages."

The aggregate age of the Class at graduation was about 2112 years.

The average age of the Class at graduation was about 22 years.

## III. TIME OF ENTRANCE.

*At the commencement of the course.*—Arnot, Bailey, G. P. Barker, A. J. Bartholomew, N. Bartholomew, Brandon, Brockway, H. B. Brown, Buehler, Bushee, Campbell, Catlin, Champlin, Clark, Coit, Condit, Cowles, Denniston, Depew, DuBois, Dunbar, Dunham, Dunlap, Eakin, C. Fellowes, Fiske, French, Gay, Hall, Harriott, Hoppin, Johnson, Keeler, Kinzer, Kittredge, Lamson, Lawrence, Lemée, McIntire, Magruder, Mann, Martin, Mills, Morse, Nettleton, Packard, Paine, Pardee, Pease, Peck, Pinneo, Price, Rackleff, Shaw, Smith, Steinman, Swift, Taylor, Turner, E. A. Walker, Webb, Whitney, Wilcox, Wilkinson, Williams, Wood, Woods, Worrall.—68.

*During Freshman year.*—Calkins, Righter, Robinson.—3.

*Sophomore year.*—Baker, T. Brown, Dickinson, Dow, Finlay, Fischer, Hodge, King, Richardson, Robbins, Southmayd, Swayne, Town.—13.

*Junior year.*—B. F. Barker, Brewer, J. M. Brown, Bulkeley, Dorrance, F. Fellowes, Harris, Monteith, Morehead, A. H. Walker, Wooton.—11.

*Senior year.*—Stickney.—1.

| | | Freshman y'r. | Soph. y'r. | Jun. y'r. | Sen. |
|---|---|---|---|---|---|
| Number in the Class | Graduates | 71 | 84 | 95 | 96 |
| | Non Graduates | 55 | 26 | 7 | 1 |
| | | 126 | 110 | 102 | 97 |
| The number that left | | 33 | 21 | 6 | 1 |
| The number that joined | | | 17 | 13 | 1 |
| Number of Graduates | | | | | 96 |
| Number of Non Graduates | | | | | 61 |
| | | | | Total, | 157. |

## IV. PROFESSIONS.†

*Clerical.*—Baker, *B. F. Barker*, *T. Brown*. Bushee, Calkins, Clark, *DuBois*, Martin, *Monteith*, Packard, Paine, Pinneo, *Robbins*, *Robinson*, Smith, *Taylor*, Town, *E. A. Walker*, Wilcox, Williams.—20.

*Exact date of birth not given.

† Those whose names are in Italics have been licensed to preach or practice.

*Legal.—G. P. Barker, A. J. Bartholomew, N. Bartholomew, Brewer,* H. B. Brown, *J. M. Brown, Bulkeley, Champlin, Coit, Condit, Denniston,* Dorrance, *Depew, Dickinson, C. E. Fellowes, F. Fellowes, Finlay,* Fischer, *Fiske, French, Hoppin,* King, *Kinzer, Kittredge, Lemée, McIntire,* Magruder, *Mann, Mills, Morehead,* Nettleton, Pardee, *Pease, Peck,* Price, *Rackleff,* Richardson, Righter, Shaw, *Steinman, Stickney, Swayne, Turner, A. H. Walker, Woods, Wooton.*     46

*Medical.*—Cowles, Dow, Hodge,     3

*Teachers.*—Harris, Johnson, Keeler, Swift, Webb, Wilkinson,     6

*Editors.*—Buehler, Morse,     2

*Civil Engineers.*—Gay, Harriott, Worrall.     3

*Mercantile.*—Arnot, Campbell, Catlin, Southmayd, Whitney, Wood,     6

*Banking.*—Dunlap, Hall,     2

*Farming.*—Bailey, Brandon, Dunbar, Eakin, Lawrence,     5

*Music.*—Dunham,     1

*Tanning.*—Lamson,     1

*Unknown.*—Brockway,     1

    96

H. B. Brown, Mann, Packard, Pinneo, Price, Shaw and Walker, have travelled in Europe; the last three are there now.

Monteith and Robbins have been ordained.

## V. MARRIED.

Bailey, Dickinson, Dunham, Eakin, Harris, Keeler, Robbins, Robinson, Taylor, Wilkinson.—10.

BORN.—A daughter to Eakin, Dec. 3, 1857; a daughter to Keeler, Oct. 2, 1858; son to Dunham, June 1858; daughter to Wilkinson, May 12, 1859; daughter to Dunham, June 27, 1859.

## VI. DECEASED.

None of the members of the Class.

Infant son of Dunham, and infant daughter of Wilkinson.

Mrs. Julia A. Wilkinson died of Pneumonia, at Washington, May 14, 1859.

## VII. MASTERS OF ARTS.

The following members took the degree of A. M., at the commencement of 1859:—B. F. Barker, Brewer, Buehler, Bulkeley, Catlin, Dunlap, Gay, Harris, Hoppin, Harriott, Hodge, Keeler, Lamson, Monteith, Morse, Packard, Paine, Pardee, Rackleff, Righter, Steinman, Turner, Webb, Wilcox, Williams, Woods. Worrall.—27.

# RECORD

## WHO LEFT THE CLASS OF 1856 WITHOUT GRADUATING.

### GEORGE BLAGDEN BACON.

Born at New Haven, Conn., May 23, 1836. Entered Freshman, from New Haven, Sept. 15, 1852. Left Nov, 15. 1853. Engaged in reporting for newspapers, &c., till April, 1856. Appointed Capt's. Clerk of the U. S. ship Portsmouth, April 5, 1856, and Acting Purser of the same ship, April 1, 1857. Held the latter office till March 15, 1858. Cruising two years in the E. I., China and Japan seas. Returned to the U. S., overland route, through Egypt and Europe, in Spring of 1858. Has "seen Paine." Is now a member of the Yale Theological Seminary.

### AUGUSTUS FIELD BEARD.

Entered Sept. 6, 1852, from South Norwalk. Left Dec. 21, 1852. Entered and graduated with the Class of 1857 at Yale. After graduating, studied Theology at Auburn. Is now in Europe.

### CODDINGTON BILLINGS.

Born at New London, Conn., Feb. 8, 1834. Connected with the Class of 1855, Yale. Entered Oct. 17, 1853. Left Nov. '53. Never recited with the Class. Married at Stonington, to Miss Mary Williams, Nov. 15, 1855 ; has one child, Coddington Billings, Jr., born Sept. 3, 1856. Residing at Stonington, Conn.

### JOHN MILTON BURRALL.

Born at South Canaan, Conn., Aug 20, 1834. Entered from Bridgeport, Conn., July 28, 1852. Left in March, 1854. Went west in Oct. 1854. In the employ of the Illinois Central Railroad about two years at Galena, Ill ; then eighteen months at Chicago, as cashier in the freight office of the same company. At present in Lakeville, Conn.

### SMITH SAMUEL CALDWELL.

Born at Marion, N. Y., 1835. Entered Oct. 16, 1852. Left Dec.

21, 1852. Entered Hamilton College, suspended, &c. Entered and graduated with the class of 1857 at Union College.

### BLAISE CARMICK CENAS.

Born at New Orleans, Feb. 26, 1836. Entered July 26, 1852. Left May 25, 1853. Has been engaged in commercial affairs at New Orleans, since leaving the Class.

### MATTHEW CHALMERS.

Entered Sept. 14, 1852. Left Dec. 21, 1852. Entered and graduated with the Class of 1858, at Yale.

### HENRY FRANCIS COCHRANE.

Born at Methuen, Mass. April 17, 1836. Entered Sept. 14, 1852. Left Feb. 28, 1854. Went almost immediately to Union, and graduated with the class of 1856. In Rochester Theological Seminary one year. Since then has been preaching. At present is at Hillsdale, Columbia Co., N. Y. Was married to Miss Mary E. Staunton, of Rochester, Aug. 31, 1857. Has one child, Frederick, born Aug. 1858.

### JOHN BELLFIELD COLLINS.

Entered Oct. 16, 1852, from Glasgow, Mo. Left Dec. 21, 1852.

### JOSEPH COLT.

Born at Palmyra, N. Y., Nov. 12, 1835. Entered Sept. 14, 1853. Left at the end of Junior year. Lived in Milwaukie as General Ticket Agent of the Milwaukie and Watertown Railroad, 1855–56. Was teller in the Bank of Commerce 1856–57. Was in New York as Transfer Clerk of the La Crosse and Milwaukie Railroad, 1857–58. Residing in Milwaukie as Teller in the Banking House of Hathaway & Belden, 1858–59.

### JOHN HENDERSON DORRISS.

Entered Oct. 9, 1852, from Platt City, Mo. Left Nov. 1852. Is said to be dead.

### LEWIS LUDLAM DUNBAR.

Born May 6, 1837, at New Bedford, Mass. Entered Sept. 14, 1852, from New Bedford. Left first term Senior year. Is now a resident of Hanover, Germany. Was married in 1858 to the daughter of a clergyman in Heelsede. Has one son born in the spring of 1859.

### LAWSON LEWIS DUNCAN.

Born at New Orleans, La., Nov. 19, 1833. Entered from New Orleans, July 26, 1852. Left Feb. 6, 1854. Studied awhile at Andover, Mass. Was a member of the University of Va., eight months. Spent the summer of 1855 in New Haven. Was in the Drug business in New York about eighteen months. In Nov. 1858, made arrangements to engage in planting near Baton Rouge, but was driven off by the Yellow Fever; "just my luck." June '58, began to study Law in Louisville, Ky. Became a partner in the Law firm of Worthington, Johnston & Duncan, in Louisville, Ky., Jan. 1, 1859.

### JOHN BLANCHARD FISHER.

Born at LaGrange, Genesee Co., N. Y., Nov. 20, 1834. Entered July 26, 1852, from Hamilton, C. W. Left June 22, 1853. Was in Rochester University one year. When at home, on a vacation, he died of the cholera, Aug. 14, 1854.

### THOMAS WILLIAM FOX.

Born at Worcester, Mass., May 24, 1835. Entered July 26, 1852. Left Dec. 21, 1852. Graduated at Brown in 1856. Studied in Harvard Law School eighteen months. Was admitted to the Bar at Boston, Jan. 1859. Practicing Law in Worcester, Mass.

### GEORGE F. FULLER.

Born in Brighton, Mass., Feb. 15, 1834. Entered July 27, 1852, from Brighton. Left Jan. 12, 1854. The first year after leaving College was engaged engineering in Illinois; the second year was an architect in Davenport, Iowa; third year was of the firm of C. K. Kirby & Co., architects, Boston. Since Jan. 1859, has been in the employ of N. J. Bradlee, architect, Brighton, Mass.

### DANIEL A. GLEASON.

Born at Worcester, Mass., May 9, 1836. Entered from Worcester, July 26, 1852. Left Dec. 21, 1852. Entered Harvard and graduated with the Class of 1856. Has been studying Law and teaching the present year at Meadville, Pa.

### JOSEPH NEWTON HALLOCK.

Born at Franklinville, L. I., July 4, 1832. Entered from Franklinville, Sept. 15, 1852. Left at the end of Junior year. Graduated with the Class of 1857, Yale. In Yale Theological Seminary, '57–59.

### JOHN WILLIAM HAMMOND.

Entered July 27, 1852, from Monticello, N. Y. Left Dec. 21, 1852.

### DAVID LLOYD HAUN.

Entered Sept. 15, 1852, from Georgetown, Ky. Left Oct. 1852.

### ANDREW FERGUSON HAYNES.

Entered Sept. 25, 1854, from New Orleans. Left Dec. 1854. Immediately after leaving College, became clerk of Payne & Harrison, Cotton Factors, N. O. April 1, 1858, became a member of the same firm, under the name of Broadwell & Haynes.

### NATHAN L. HAZEN.

Born at Worthington, Mass., April 1, 1832. Entered Sept. 15, 1852, from Worthington, Mass. Left Dec. 21, 1852. Spent two years in recovering his eyesight. Has been engaged in farming since Oct. 1856, at Sydney, Champaign Co., Ill.

### CHAUNCEY RUSSELL HUBBARD.

Born at New Haven, Aug, 11, 1835. Entered from New Haven, July 26, 1852. Left Dec. 21, 1852. Was in the Lumber business at New Haven, in the employ of William Jumper, till July 1855, when he was engaged in the foundry of Stevens & Co., at Middletown, Conn. Sailed for Paria, Brazil, March 16, 1856, as agent of Hotchkiss & Everett, of New Haven, and died of Yellow Fever eleven days after his arrival, May 2, 1856.

### WILLIAM EDWARD HULBERT.

Born at Middletown, Conn., May 19, 1834. Entered from New Haven, Sept. 14, 1852. Left at close of the second term Sophomore year. Taught in Wm. H. Russell's school till Sept. 1855, when he joined the Class of '57 and graduated with that Class. Since graduating has been teaching in Mr. Russell's school.

### PARMENAS B. HULSE.

Born at Rome, N. Y., May 6, 1829. Entered from Port Jervis, N. Y., Sept. 15, 1852. Left third term Sophomore year. Was principal of Woodbury Academy, Aug. 1854 to May 1856. Principal of the High School at Ansonia, May '56—May '57. Principal of High School, and Superintendent of Public Schools in Waterbury, '57—'59. Was married to Miss Catherine Smith of Woodbury, Aug. 1856. Has one child, Cornelia Louisa, born April, 1859.

### SYLVESTER HUNT.

Born at Woodbury, Conn., Oct. 19, 1830. Entered from Woodbury, July, 26, 1852. Left Dec. 21, 1852. Spent two years in travelling for his health. Was engaged in teaching till 1858, since which time he has been farming at Wenona, Ill. Was married to Miss Emma McAllen, of Wenona, June 14, 1858.

### MOSES BROWN JENKINS.

Entered from Providence, R. I., July 27, 1852. Left Dec. 21, '52. Graduated as a partial course man, at Brown University, 1855.

### JOHN E. KIMBALL.

Born at Webster, Mass., July 18, 1833. Entered from Oxford, Mass., July 26, 1852. Left July 22, 1853. Entered and graduated with the Class of 1858, at Yale. Has since been at home, (Oxford,) teaching in the Winter.

### DAVID BRADLEY LEE.

Entered from New York City, July 26, 1852. Left Jan. 8, 1853. Said to be in Paris.

### JAMES TURNER LEFTWICH.

Entered from Liberty, Va., Oct. 18, 1852. Left Feb. 3, 1854. Graduated at Princeton, in 1856. Graduated at Union Theological Seminary, in 1859, and is now preaching in Virginia.

### WILLIAM ALEXANDER MAGILL.

Born in Bryan Co., Ga., Jan. 2, 1836. Entered from Waterbury, Conn., July 26, 1852. Left Jan. 31, 1854. Clerked it three months. Was assistant in Waterbury High School one year. Returned to Yale in the Summer of 1855, and graduated with the Class of 1858. After graduating he taught four months in an Academy at Middlebury, Conn., thence went as a teacher to Westerly, R. I. Post office address, Pawcatuck Village, Conn.

### FARNCIS FREEMAN MARSHALL.

Born at Girard, Erie Co., Pa., May 21, 1836. Entered from Erie Pa., Sept. 14th, 1852. Left, Nov. 1853. Immediately entered his father's office. Was admitted to the Bar Oct., 1857. Is practicing Law in partnership with his father at Erie, Pa.

### DANIEL MERRITT MEAD.

Born at Greenwich, Conn., June 2, 1834. Entered from Greenwich, July 26, 1852. Left, Feb. 8, 1854. Was admitted to the Bar of New York, Aug., 1855, and to the Bar of Conn., March, 1856. Was married to Miss Louisa T. Mead, of Greenwich, June 16th, 1856. He is practicing Law at Greenwich.

### ROBERT JAMES V. MEECH.

Entered from Albany, Sept. 14th, 1852. Left at the end of Freshman year. Is said to have been connected with the office of the New York Times.

### ALMON BAXTER MERWIN.

Born at Brooklyn, L. I., June 27, 1835. Entered from N. Y., July 27, 1852. Left Oct. 4, 1853. Graduated at Yale with the Class of 1857. After graduating, was in Union Theo. Sem., from Sept. '57, to Feb. '58, when he left on account of ill health. Since then engaged in teaching.

### SAMUEL TRACY COIT MERWIN.    *

Born in Brooklyn, L. I., Nov. 16, 1835. Entered from Norwich, Conn., Sept. 14, 1852. Was a devotee of the Field Sports of America till May 20, 1858, when he commenced the study of law, at Norwich, Conn.

### EDWIN HARRISON MILLER.

Born at Williamsburg, Mass., Sept. 2, 1833. Entered from Williamsburg, Oct. 11th, 1852. Left July 22, 1853. Has been sea-faring since. Has made a voyage around the world. Is now supposed to be at Carthagena.

### EUGENE POPE MOORE.

Born at Frankfort, Ky., July 12th, 1837. Entered from Frankfort, Sept. 13th, 1854. Left 2d term, Junior year. Graduated at Montrose Law College, May 17th, 1858. Licensed to practice, July, 1858. Admitted to the Bar at Frankfort, March, 1859.

### SIDNEY ASH MOULTHROP.

Born at Orange, Conn., Jan. 10, 1833. Entered from New Haven, July 26, 1852. Left July 22, 1853. Was in the Class of 1857 during Freshman year. Was engaged in the Town Clerk's office at New Haven and in teaching music, till July, 1858. Entered New Haven Law School in the fall of 1857. Will probably be admitted to the Bar this fall.

### ROBERT LEYBURN MUENCH.

Entered, Sept. 15, 1852, from Harrisburg, Pa. Left April 12, 1853. Is practicing Law at Harrisburg.

### CYRUS NORTHROP.

Born at Ridgefield, Ct., Sept. 30, 1836. Entered from Ridgefield, July 28th, 1852. Left on account of ill health, in May, 1853. Joined and graduated with the Class of 1857, at Yale. Since graduating, has been a member of Yale Law School and engaged in teaching. Received the degree of L. L. B., July, 1859. Intends to study awhile in the office of Chas. Ives, Esq., New Haven, and to practice in Conn-

### JAMES PARSONS.

Entered from Hartford, Conn., Jan. 6, 1853. Left at the close of Freshman year.

### SAMUEL CALVIN PECK.

Born at Greenwich, Conn., Aug. 21, 1834. Entered from Greenwich, July 26, 1852. Left at the end of first term, Sophomore year. I can give only a mere outline of a long and interesting letter from his brother. He was Superintendent of the Greenwich Public Schools nine months. His health not improving, in 1854 he shipped before the mast, in a vessel bound from Boston to California, Sandwich Islands, and China. Receiving no benefit from the voyage, he left the vessel at Valparaiso. He worked his way home through great hardships, and arrived after an absence of six months. He then joined a corps of engineers on the Superior Railroad, and while absent from the corps, was taken down with the typhus fever, and was found by his friends in the cabin of a German backwoodsman. He was removed to Greenwich, but soon sank into a state of insensibility, in which he lay over two weeks, and died Sept. 23, 1857. " At the early age of eleven years, he had united with the church, and his after-walk was consistent with his profession."

### WINSLOW LEWIS PERKINS.

Born at New London, Conn., Dec. 8,1835. Entered from New London, July 17, 1852. Left Dec. 21, 1852. Traveled in Europe, and since his return has studied medicine mostly at home.

### HORTON REYNOLDS PLATT.

Born at Southeast, N. Y., Aug. 15, 1834. Entered from White Plains, July 28, 1852. Left Sophomore year. Immediately entered the Law School at Poughkeepsie, N. Y., for one term. Admitted to practice, April 8, 1856, since which time he has been practicing Law at White Plains, N. Y.

### JULIEN TERRELL RANSONE.

Entered from Sparta, Ga., July 26, 1852. Left Dec. 21, 1852. Joined the class of 1857, left it in Junior year. At present in Berkeley, Early Co., Ga.

### CHARLES PRESCOTT SANBORN.

Entered from Concord, N. H., Sept. 14, 1852. Left July 20, 1855. Since leaving has been teaching and studying Law at Concord.

### FRANKLIN SIDWAY.

Born at Buffalo, N. Y., July 23, 1834. Entered from Buffalo, July 27, 1852. Left April 1, 1853. After leaving he traveled in Europe a year and a half. Has been engaged in the ship chandlery business at Buffalo three years. Sold out in the Spring of 1859.

### EDWARD PAYSON SMITH.

Born at Granby, Mass., Sept. 3, 1832. Entered from Enfield, Mass., July 28, 1852. Left Dec. 21, 1852. Was married to Miss Charlotte Woods, daughter of Hon. J. B. Woods, of Enfield, Oct. 31, 1855. Is a merchant at Enfield.

### ISRAEL SELDEN SPENCER.

Entered from Port Gibson, Miss., Oct. 17, 1853. Left during Sophomore year. Joined the class of 1857, but left before graduating.

### GEORGE BUCKINGHAM ST. JOHN.

Born at Norwalk, Conn., Sept. 14, 1832. Entered with the class. Left at the end of Junior year. Has since been residing in Norwalk.

### THOMAS THAXTER.

Born at Methuen, Mass., Dec., 24, 1833. Entered from Methuen, Sept. 14, 1852. Left at the close of second term, Sophomore year. Graduated at Harvard in 1856. Since graduating, has been teaching, as health would permit. For the last few months has been in Minnesota, trying to recover from the effects of a fever, and teaching at Stillwater.

### JOHN DARIUS TOMLINSON.

Born at Woodbury, Conn., Oct. 12, 1835. Was connected with the class of 1855, at Yale. Entered Oct. 12, 1853. Left in Nov. 1853. Died of consumption at Woodbury, June 20, 1854.

### SAMUEL MAVERICK VAN WYCK.

Born in 1855. Entered from Pendleton, S. C., July 27, 1852. Left July 22, 1853. Engaged in the tanning business in the mountainous district of South Carolina, from June 1854, to March 1858. Has been studying medicine since May 1, 1858, and attending lectures in New York. Expects a diploma in the Spring of 1860. Was married in the Spring of 1855, to Miss Margaret C. Broyles, daughter of Dr. R. Broyles, of South Carolina. Has been blessed with three boys, William, born at Williamston, S. C., March 8, 1856. Samuel, born at the same place, April 1, 1857. Ozé, born at Anderson, S. C., Aug. 1, 1858.

### THOMAS WARD.

Entered from Fayette, Mo., Sept. 14, 1852. Left Feb. 1854. Remained home till the fall of 1857. Made several trips to "Bleeding Kansas," and in one trip was accidentally one of Reid's grand army. Was married to Miss Alice Talbott, of Fayette Co., Sept. 3, 1857. Has had one son, Thomas, born Aug. 29, 1858.

### JOHN WILLIAM WEEMS.

Born in Maryland, Oct. 10, 1835. Connected with Bethany College, Va. Entered Jan. 11, 1853, from Alexandres, La. Left at the close of Freshman year. Was a resident student of Medicine, in the Charity Hospital, in New Orleans, La. Was shot by a law student, at New Orleans, and died, Feb. 2, 1858.

### GEORGE WAKEMAN WHEELER.

Born at Easton, Conn., Oct. 15, 1834. Connected with the Class of 1855. Entered the Class of 1856, Sept. 15, 1852, from Easton. Left May 4, 1853. Graduated at Amherst with the Class of 1856. Occupied since in teaching school.

### WILLARD WETMORE WHITE.

Born at New Haven, Feb. 7, 1836. Entered from New Haven, July 26, 1852. Left Dec. 21, 1852. Remained in New Haven five or six months. January 1853, went to New York in the employ of T. B. Coddington & Co., dealers in Hardware. Remains there at present.

### CHARLES HENRY SOMERS WILLIAMS.

Born at Cazenovia, N. Y., Oct. 7, 1836. Entered Jan. 6, 1853. Left April 1, 1854. Spent two years at Union, and graduated there in Sept. 1856. Was in the Law School at Poughkeepsie about ten months; traveling in the North-west about two months. In Jan. 1858, entered a Law office in New York; remained there eight months. Then removed to Poughkeepsie, and is now a member of the law firm of Smith & Williams, 48 Market street, Poughkeepsie.

### HOWARD CORNELIUS WILLIAMS.

Born Jan. 28, 1836. Entered July 27, 1852, from Ithaca, N. Y. Left Nov. 3, 1852. Joined the Class of 1857, but did not graduate with them. Graduated at some other college in '57. Since then has been engaged in the flour business.

9

### LUCIEN BONAPARTE WOOLFOLK.

Entered Sept. 14, 1852, from Trimble Co. Ky. Left July 24, 1853. Was in Brown University a short time.

---

## THE CLASS VINE.

Planted June 19, 1856. In 1857 it was cut down by the mowers, and again in 1858. This summer I have digged about it, and now it is growing again finely.